CU00922522

MMXVI

THE WHITE REVIEW

EDITORS   BENJAMIN EASTHAM & JACQUES TESTARD
DESIGN, ART DIRECTION   RAY O'MEARA
SENIOR EDITOR   FRANCESCA WADE
US EDITOR   TYLER CURTIS
ASSISTANT EDITORS   CASSIE DAVIES, IZABELLA SCOTT
DESIGN ASSISTANT   THOM SWANN
READERS   JAMES DRANEY, CARLA MANFREDINO

MARKETING MANAGER   BERRY PATTEN

CONTRIBUTING EDITORS   JACOB BROMBERG, LAUREN ELKIN, EMMELINE FRANCIS,
                              ORIT GAT, PATRICK LANGLEY, BELLA MARRIN,
                              DANIEL MEDIN, SAM SOLNICK, EMILY STOKES,
                              J. S. TENNANT, HARRY THORNE, KISHANI WIDYARATNA

HONORARY TRUSTEES   MICHAEL AMHERST, DEREK ARMSTRONG, HUGUES DE DIVONNE,
                              SIMON FAN, NIALL HOBHOUSE, CATARINA LEIGH-PEMBERTON,
                              MICHAEL LEUE, AMY POLLNER, CÉCILE DE ROCHEQUAIRIE,
                              EMMANUEL ROMAN, HUBERT TESTARD, MICHEL TESTARD,
                              GORDON VENEKLASEN, DANIELA & RON WILLSON,
                              CAROLINE YOUNGER

BOARD OF TRUSTEES   BENJAMIN EASTHAM, TOM MORRISON-BELL, JACQUES TESTARD

THE WHITE REVIEW IS A REGISTERED CHARITY (NUMBER 1148690)

COVER ART BY MOONI PERRY
PRINTED BY PUSH, LONDON
PAPER BY ANTALIS MCNAUGHTON (OLIN CREAM 100GSM, OLIN NATURAL WHITE 120GSM)
BESPOKE PAPER MARBLE BY PAYHEMBURY MARBLE PAPERS
TYPESET IN JOYOUS (BLANCHE)

PUBLISHED BY THE WHITE REVIEW, OCTOBER 2016
EDITION OF 1,800
ISBN No. 978-0-9927562-9-1

COPYRIGHT © THE WHITE REVIEW AND INDIVIDUAL CONTRIBUTORS, 2016.
ALL RIGHTS RESERVED. NO REPRODUCTION, COPY OR TRANSMISSION,
IN WHOLE OR IN PART, MAY BE MADE WITHOUT WRITTEN PERMISSION.

THE WHITE REVIEW, 243 KNIGHTSBRIDGE, LONDON SW7 1DN
WWW.THEWHITEREVIEW.ORG

Supported using public funding by
ARTS COUNCIL
ENGLAND
LOTTERY FUNDED

EDITORIAL

IN 1992 THE POET and novelist Eileen Myles, interviewed in this eighteenth print issue of *THE WHITE REVIEW*, ran for office as President of the United States. It seems unlikely that any editor of this magazine will ever run for high office, though given the current chaos on both sides of the Atlantic it would be foolish to make any firm predictions. In the presumably permanent absence of direct legislative influence, we are faced with the increasingly pressing question of how a magazine can contribute to a democratic process which seems everywhere under threat. The temptation is to throw the meagre weight of this small institution behind policies and strategies that reflect our own convictions, and to transform it into a mouthpiece for the dissemination of ideas that collectively communicate a coherent and actionable political position.

Yet, as this country recovers from the most divisive political event in a generation, we might pause to consider the responsibilities of the magazine as a space for open dialogue. The campaign to remain in the European Union failed in large part because it presumed the self-evidence of its case and shied away from antagonistic discussion in favour of a browbeating insistence that the political establishment (and such institutions as the IMF) knew what was right for our communities. In Brexit's wake it became routine to hear expressed (and rare to hear challenged) the conviction that an outright majority of the population were incapable of making a decision in their own interests, when even the most cursory glance at that dysfunctional, autocratic union revealed good (which isn't necessarily to say sufficient) reasons for leaving. The implication that a large part of the citizenry does not deserve the franchise is deeply troubling.

In retrospect, it might be that the overwhelming consensus of literary and art establishments in opposition to Brexit was a symptom of weakness rather than strength. Our magazines and art spaces have always operated as arenas for the exchange of disruptive ideas, forums for what the political theorist Chantal Mouffe has termed the 'agonistic' practice of democracy, and it is a cause for concern when they succumb to the same narrow range of recycled opinions that we encounter through our social media feeds. Perhaps it is occasionally the responsibility of the artist, editor, curator to promote opinions that do not in fact reflect their own, to frame and instigate thought rather than guide it; perhaps we might be more conscious of our own unacknowledged prejudices. This is not to say that all opinions are equally valid, but rather that they should be refuted or rejected rather than simply suppressed.

Engagement with art and literature is one means by which we come to understand as partial and conditional our perspective on the world, and thereby to recognise that a functioning democracy depends on the accommodation of diverse opinions which might never satisfactorily be reconciled. The magazine might serve as a model, albeit on the smallest imaginable scale, for a pluralistic society in which conflicting voices can be heard and contradictory opinions expressed without any loss of legitimacy either for the project or the individual. Art can, as the novelist and activist Garth Greenwell recently pointed out in an interview for THE WHITE REVIEW, enable an 'empathy' that carries a deeper, though less immediate, political effect than that which is achievable through wrangling over policy. In the variety of aesthetics, conceptual preoccupations, styles and themes gathered within these pages we hope the reader will be introduced to new ways of thinking about the world, and discover some means by which we might change it.

THE EDITORS

AT THE CLINIC

BY

SALLY ROONEY

ON THE WAY to the dental clinic they talk about going home for Christmas. It's November and Marianne is having a wisdom tooth removed. Connell is driving her to the clinic because he's her only friend with a car, and also the only person in whom she confides about distasteful medical conditions like impacted teeth. He sometimes drives her to the doctor's office when she needs antibiotics for urinary tract infections, which is often. They are 23.

Connell parks up around the corner from the clinic and the radio switches itself off. He has taken the morning off work to drive Marianne to the appointment, which he hasn't told her. He's doing it partly out of guilt. A week previously Marianne gave him head in his apartment and complained afterwards that her jaw hurt, and he was like, do you have to complain about everything all the time? Then they argued. They were both a little drunk.

Marianne remembers the incident differently. She remembers giving Connell head for a while on his sofa and then she stopped because her mouth hurt. He was pretty nice about it and they had sex on the couch instead. Only afterwards, when she started talking about her mouth again, did Connell say: You complain a lot more than other people. They were lying side by side on the sofa then. Marianne said, you mean your other girlfriends. And Connell said no, he meant people, as in everyone. He said no one he knew in any capacity complained as much as Marianne.

You don't like hearing people complain because you're incapable of expressing sympathy, Marianne said.

I already told you I was sorry the first time you complained.

You like women who don't complain because you don't want to see women as fully human.

Every time I criticise you, it turns into a thing about me hating women, he said.

Marianne started to sit up then. She gathered her hair into a roll and felt for a clip to put through it.

I find it suspicious, she said. That you always get into relationships with people you don't actually talk to.

You're upset and you're taking it out on me now, he said. I'm not completely stupid.

She touched her hair with her hands to feel that it was in place and then lay back down beside him. It was a bad sofa, with a pattern of brown flowers.

Me, she said. You see me as a full human being. That's why you're not attracted to me.

Yes I am.

Sexually, but not romantically.

She watched him looking up at the ceiling then. Their faces were very close together.

I guess if it was romantic I wouldn't like you having other boyfriends, he said.

F

Although actually, you don't.

I don't like your taste in boyfriends, that's different.

Do you want to know what happened with Daniel? she said. I told him I had a dream about getting married and he said, to me? And I said no, to my friend Connell. The rest of the argument wasn't about you, it was about how I say things purposely to bother him because I enjoy making him feel bad about himself.

Oh.

Marianne went home after that, wondering if she complained too much. By the time she got back to her apartment her whole head was aching. She took a bottle of gin from the inside of the fridge door and poured a little into her mouth experimentally. Rinsing the cold alcohol around her gums, a gigantic pain shot up the inside of her jaw and made her eyes water. She drooled the gin back out into the kitchen sink and started crying.

She went to the dental clinic on her own the next morning. On the way there she planned sensationalist things she could tell the dentist about the pain in her jaw. It's not that bad most of the time, she imagined herself saying, but giving blowjobs is out of the question. Instead the dentist took a quick look at her mouth and prescribed a round of antibiotics for what he called a 'truly nasty' infection. I'm not surprised you're in pain, the dentist said. That tooth is slicing through your cheek like butter. He scribbled something on a notepad and then looked up at her. Once the infection's come down we'll take it out for you no problem, he said. You won't know yourself. Marianne takes significant personal pleasure in having her pain validated by professionals.

They are now the only two people in the upstairs waiting room of the dental clinic. The seats are a pale mint-green colour. Marianne leafs through an issue of NATIONAL GEOGRAPHIC and explores her mouth with the tip of her tongue. Connell looks at the magazine cover, a photograph of a monkey with huge eyes. That night last week, Marianne had called him first to tell him that she and Daniel had broken up. Connell was in the bathroom when the phone rang and his flatmate Barry answered. When Connell came back, Barry said innocently: Hey, what's the name of that rich girl you went to school with? You know, the one you like to fuck. Believing the query was sincere, Connell replied: Marianne, why? Then Barry tossed him the phone. She wants to talk to you, he said. When Connell lifted the phone he could already hear her laughing.

In the waiting room Connell is thinking about Lauren, his girlfriend of nearly ten months. She moved to Manchester in September and two weeks ago she slept with someone else when she was drunk. When she told him about it, his failure to feel anything unnerved him and he wondered whether he cared about her at all. For a few days he felt vaguely depressed and tired, and then he slept with Marianne, who accused him of not seeing women as 'full human beings'. He realised then that he did not in fact see Lauren as a 'full human being', but as a minor character in his own life. For this reason, what she did offstage didn't matter to him. After Marianne left that night, he opened a new tab on his browser and typed: why can I not feel things.

The next morning, he called Lauren on Skype and told her he thought they should break up. She agreed with him, non-committally. We had fun, she said, but the long-distance thing was never going to work. This sketched trajectory of their relationship bore so little resemblance to anything he thought or felt that he just nodded and said: Yeah, exactly. He has not yet told Marianne about this Skype conversation. She's had the whole drama with her tooth going on and he doesn't want it to look like he made a major decision as a result of sleeping with her. Like butter, she says every time they talk. I'm in agony. Connell has actually missed the original import of the butter simile and now decides it's late enough that he can ask.

What's this butter thing you keep talking about? he says.

My cheek being like butter.

Your what? he says.

Remember the dentist said, that tooth is slicing through your cheek like butter.

Connell stares at her over the yellow rim of her magazine.

Fuck, it's physically slicing through your cheek? he says.

Have you not been listening to me? I've been talking about it for like a week.

I think I must tune you out sometimes.

She gazes back into the magazine, looking amused.

A life skill, she says.

So you know, I broke up with Lauren. I don't know if you heard that.

For a moment she pretends to be engaged in reading. He can see she's deciding what to do or say. The workings of Marianne's mind become transparent to him in brief flashes like this before they recede again.

You didn't mention, she says.

Yeah, well.

He coughs, though he doesn't need to. This is a weakness and he knows that Marianne senses it, like blood in water.

When did all this go down? she says.

About a week ago.

Aha.

She doesn't perform the 'aha'. She just closes the magazine and puts it back on the small glass table in one languid gesture. Connell swallows. What is he swallowing for? In school Marianne was ugly and everyone hated her. He likes to think about this sadistically when he feels she's getting the better of him in conversation. In their last year of school he took her virginity and then asked her not to tell people, although he doesn't actually feel very good about that any more. She just lay there like: Why would I want to tell anyone? He finds this emblematic of something.

Marianne feels humiliated that Connell hasn't told her about Lauren until now. She disguises these feelings by focusing a slow disdainful attention on her immediate surroundings. She wonders if Connell hasn't told her because he finds her desperate. As a 23-year-old Marianne is occasionally subject to the same dismal anxieties that characterised her adolescent life. Throughout school she was contemptuous of others, but simultaneously seized by a fear of other people's contempt. Connell was the first person who really liked her, and even he wouldn't speak to her in front of his friends. She did degrading things to retain his affection and pretended not to find them degrading. She stayed quiet in the background of his phone calls.

Yeah, I thought you would have heard, he says. It was one of these Skype break-ups. Relatively relaxed as break-ups go.

Lauren's a relaxed girl.

That's probably true.

He looks out of the window and attempts to yawn. He hates himself. He has no idea what Marianne is thinking. Compulsively and out of self-directed spite he thinks about the fact that all the time he and Lauren were together, he never made her come except by accident. With Marianne he has always found it gorgeously, stupidly easy. Of course he knows this means nothing.

Well, don't worry, Marianne says. I know we're both single now, but I'm not going to ask you to be my boyfriend.

Weirdly enough I wasn't worrying about that.

The door opens then and a nurse comes out saying: Marianne? We're ready for you. Marianne looks at Connell, and he looks back at her. Momentarily she hates him but the malice always dissipates. He doesn't mean to touch this terrible need in her. With Daniel she felt so free and empowered, because she never took him seriously. His desire to hurt her only emphasised how much he relied on her. But Connell needs nothing and with him she feels powerless. She touches a hand to her face and follows the nurse into the surgery.

When the door closes, Connell gets up and walks to the window. He looks out over the street, at the tops of people's heads going by. It's a clear day, cold and blue like an ice pop. He's trying not to think about Marianne in pain. He knows they'll numb the necessary part of her mouth, but this agitates him also. Marianne doesn't express fear of physical suffering. Connell has seen bad things happen to her. Still, it hurt him when she said she didn't want to be his girlfriend, partly because of how gratuitous it was. He was never going to ask her anyway. He starts to chew on his thumbnail, until he can feel it become pulpy and twisted in his mouth.

When he first heard she'd finally broken up with Daniel, he was just happy for

F

her. Daniel was one of these skinny graphic designers who wore thick-framed glasses and talked about gender a lot. Connell sat beside him in the bar at Marianne's birthday and in lieu of conversation they watched the Bournemouth-Chelsea game on the big screen. Daniel asked: Does it really matter who wins or loses? Well kind of, said Connell. Bournemouth go back into the relegation zone if they lose this one. I meant on a philosophical level, Daniel said. That was a real conversation that happened between them. Daniel was laughing and saying: Masculinity is a fragile thing. Connell didn't bring up some things he happened to know about Daniel's proclivities. You're the one who likes to tie her up and hit her with a belt, he didn't say. I bet that makes you feel like a big guy.

Inside the surgery they have given Marianne an anaesthetic. The dentist sticks a sharp instrument into her gum to see if she can feel it, and she can't. Then he sets about removing the tooth. At first she can hear grinding. A glowing white lamp reflects into her eyes from the mirror above her, and the latex of the dentist's gloves tastes sadomasochistic. Something is whirring, and a strange thin liquid is filling Marianne's mouth. It does not taste like blood. Then she feels something slip down onto her tongue, something smooth and heavy, and suddenly she is sitting upright and the dentist is saying: Spit it out! She spits something into the dentist's hand. It is a small yellow part of her own body. Now she can taste blood, and something else. Her head hurts. The tooth glistens like cream in the dentist's palm. Good woman, the dentist says. The tooth has fronds like an anemone. Marianne is trembling.

Connell is afraid that he is an emotionally empty person. He tries to look at the issue of NATIONAL GEOGRAPHIC on the table, but he lacks focus and thinks recurrently about Marianne's pain. Marianne involves herself in things that are bad for her. That's an opinion Connell has that he feels guilty about. He knows that she attracts blame for things that aren't her fault simply because of her tough personality. People have taken advantage of Marianne, but maybe she allowed that to continue when it didn't have to. She told him some of the things Daniel made her do. She showed him things. I know it's kind of fucked up, she said. I don't enjoy it. And she laughed, he hated that she laughed.

The dentist packs Marianne's mouth with gauze and gets her to bite down. She's feeling woozy, as though the tooth is a sick child she has given birth to. She remembers that Connell is in the waiting room and feels a tidal gratitude which drenches her in sweat. The gauze rubs her numbed tongue and her eyes begin to prick with tears. The medical part of the procedure is over now. They scoop her out of the chair as if she's a piece of newspaper.

The surgery door opens and Connell turns from the window. Marianne points idiotically at her mouth. They have given her the tooth in a jar and she rattles it at him. Her face is lopsided and misshapen like a deflating tent. He experiences certain

F

feelings. In school he used to fantasise about making intellectual or witty remarks in front of Marianne. It's a fantasy he still engages in compulsively during moments of stress. Her imaginary laughter soothes his nerves.

Are you all finished then? he says.

She nods, she tries to swallow. Her mouth feels wrong, she's in the wrong body.

That was fast, he says. How are you feeling?

She shrugs. She feels the shudder that precipitates a sob and tries to repress this particular kind of ugliness. It's too late. She's crying. Clumsily she rubs her eyes, her nose, the numb abyss of her right cheek. She shrugs again. At least the crying is silent.

Connell has only seen Marianne crying once before, when they were teenagers. Her mother had a boyfriend then, called Steven. He came into Marianne's room at night sometimes to 'talk'. She went to Connell's house one night after it happened and she cried and said: Sometimes I think I deserve bad things because I'm a bad person. He had never heard anyone talk like that. He felt sick, and from that moment the sick– ness would always be there, even if he couldn't feel it. It was outside him then.

Let's get in the car, he says.

In the car she's small and lonely. In one hand she's holding the jar with her tooth in it, and in the other hand she has a small roll of replacement gauze for her mouth. Placing both items into her lap carefully she reaches for the visor above her seat to look in the mirror.

I wouldn't necessarily, he says.

She pauses with her hand on the mirror.

Do I look that bad? she says.

Her voice is muffled and thick.

You don't look bad to me, he says, but you seem fragile now and I don't want you freaking out.

At first he thinks Marianne is coughing, but then he realises he's making her laugh.

So I look bad, she says. Why didn't you tell me about Lauren?

He kneads the steering wheel under his hands. She watches him. She darts away the threat of a tear from her left eye, discreetly, with her sleeve.

This little speech you gave me, he says. About seeing women as human beings. It kind of disturbed me actually.

What, and that's why you broke up with her?

In some complex way this question, combined with the fact that Marianne is vis– ibly crying, excites him. He thinks, involuntarily, of her naked body. He considers it an image of vulnerability rather than something sexual, but it feels like both. He knows that she's crying simply from a residual physical pain, which he doesn't take any pleasure in. But her desire to be cared for touches him. A fantasy that beneath her cold exterior there's something else.

She notices that he doesn't immediately answer her question. He's watching the traffic as if he's thinking of something else. She hopes that her brash curiosity appears dismissive. This is one of many dynamic strategies she employs to conceal from Connell what she feels for him. What she feels is not easily expressed anyway. People love all kinds of things: their friends, their parents. Misunderstandings are inevitable.

You're still crying, are you? he says.

The feeling is coming back now, she says. That's all.

INTERVIEW

WITH

EILEEN MYLES

I sat across from Eileen Myles at a large empty table in her London publisher's office a few hours before a sold out reading at the Serpentine Gallery. I ask her about her plans for after our interview, wondering how to begin. She shrugs. 'More of the same.'

Over the last twelve months, following the reissue of her out-of-print 1994 autobiographical novel CHELSEA GIRLS and the collection I MUST BE LIVING TWICE: NEW AND SELECTED POEMS 1975-2014, there has been an almost mythical resurgence in Myles's popularity. With nineteen books of poetry and prose behind her, she is not exactly news, having been active for forty years and influenced a whole generation of radical writers and activists, but the last year has been something different. From a NEW YORK TIMES profile (illustrated with an Inez and Vinoodh portrait of Myles in a Comme des Garçons jacket) to a television character based on her (played by Cherry Jones on the Amazon show TRANSPARENT), it has constituted a kind of initiation into the mainstream, one that Myles perhaps called best in her 1991 poem 'Peanut Butter': 'All / the things I / embrace as new / are in / fact old things, / re-released.' While forty years seem like a long time even for mainstream culture to catch up with what has been there all along, it is precisely the striking, almost recalcitrant consistency of her authorcharacter persona that resists assimilation. She is the opposite of seasonal.

Few artists can communicate in as bright and fluid a shorthand as Myles. There is a perpetual sense of immediacy at play, a nowness maintained by a frequency of jumping between one tense or register and another in a flickering swoop. At core prosodic, her writing is often generated by rhythms and inflections of speech, attesting to Myles's ear for a particular place and time. It is a poetry of appetites and human needs, of grandiosity and struggle, mediated through the running stream of personal experience. Her language, often simple and prosaic, seems detachable from context while held together in a self-concealing form. Attempting to pin it down is to miss the point; as Myles's 2001 poem 'Writing' begins: 'I can / connect // any two / things // that's / god // teeny piece / of bandaid.'

Her origin story is by now well-known: growing up in blue-collar Boston, she moved to the East Village of New York in 1974 to be a poet, landing straight into the poetic avant-garde epitomised by the St Mark's Church contingent and getting by with a string of odd jobs including taking care of James Schuyler at the end of his life. These early days are recounted in a number of her books, most notably CHELSEA GIRLS and INFERNO (A POET'S NOVEL), each subsequent rendering continuing Myles's practice of self-making, often to the effect of film reels overlaid on each other. It is a work of perpetual arrival, one that 'violates the hermetic nature of my own museum', as the eponymous poem in her breakthrough volume NOT ME goes.

Myles takes the antiquated baggage of confessional writing and subverts it with a supreme irreverence. It is not simply about wielding the personal in public; it's about exploring shame and powerlessness not as implications on the individual but on the culture in which she belongs. It is the inversion of what Elizabeth Hardwick wrote of the 'scolding power' of the word disgrace in female consciousness: 'It freezes the radical heart with lashing whispers.' Myles' work has always been a means to cut through the whisper, to instantly heat up the room.

––––––––––

Q. THE WHITE REVIEW — What would have been different had we done this interview a year ago? Has your increased visibility changed the way you perceive what you are doing?

A. EILEEN MYLES — I think the challenge is always to talk from where you actually are. It's always like being in a different culture. My joke has always been that if being an alcoholic didn't destroy my writing, if being a lesbian didn't destroy my writing, if being an academic didn't destroy my writing, why would…

Q. THE WHITE REVIEW — Being canonised?

A. EILEEN MYLES — Yes. In a way it's none of my business and it's a matter of figuring out how to make what I'm doing be even more intimate than it has been. I started writing in the seventies and it was very quiet and nobody gave a damn that I was writing or that I was me, and there was so much freedom in that. Lately I got an award and rather than making a speech I just read my newest poem. That felt right. That's what I mean by intimate. So there's just a way now in which maybe I can relax, and yet you don't want to relax too much. I want to be precise in this freedom.

Q. THE WHITE REVIEW — John Ashbery wrote that some artists, and possibly the best ones, pass from 'unacceptability to acceptance without an intervening period of appreciation'. Do you feel something similar can be said about the reception of your work? That in a sense, you did time?

A. EILEEN MYLES — Yes, and I mean, not until recently has the press actually gotten really smart. In terms of say, getting reviewed, what often is getting reviewed is the fact that I've become famous, and I was still not having the work be written about. THE NEW YORK TIMES had some guy who was a cultural critic writing

about me, and he talked mostly about my work in my twenties, and that I was, like, badass and punk, and I was just like, 'How is this relevant to the work I'm doing now?' But there was an amazing piece in THE NEW YORK REVIEW OF BOOKS that was beautiful and smart. Getting my work actually written about is like being loved or something. I feel like that's how I want to be seen. Meaning read.

Q. THE WHITE REVIEW — How is it that you would like to be seen now? What is different about your work now, and how do you feel about your older work?

A. EILEEN MYLES — I'm saying I'd enjoy being viewed and written about as a writer rather than as a cultural phenomenon. I think it's more sexism – to see my work being read as this raw sexual thing – which only makes editors want more of that, rather than my next book. I think being a female or a queer writer is uniquely strange because you still are all those things before the word 'writer', when in all the years you were writing that wasn't necessarily what was in the room with you. I was in my body writing. So is a man. So is anyone. So please tell me about the effect of the work, what's in it, and I don't mean content. What's the experience of reading it? That's how I write about books.

Q. THE WHITE REVIEW — In INFERNO you write that 'an artist's responsibility for a very long time is to get collected, socially'. Do you feel that to be the case for younger poets now?

A. EILEEN MYLES — I don't think I can honestly say how it is for younger poets now. I mean, their rent is higher. A younger poet more likely meets older poets in graduate programmes rather than at parties. It's a safer world in many ways, but also more economically driven, more inside, I believe.

Q. THE WHITE REVIEW — When you moved to New York, did you feel you were entering a certain tradition?

A. EILEEN MYLES — Yes, very much. St Mark's Church was an academy of sorts. It was the academy that thought of itself as connected to the art world and performance art and the history of art in America, of avant-garde art in America, and thought of itself as not academic. As soon as I got to New York, I think I had read one or two poems of Frank O'Hara's, and I remember standing in a bookstore, Corinth Books, and picking Frank O'Hara's SELECTED POEMS out of a pile and reading it. And I thought he sounded just like the city. It was this kind of gay man talking immediately, and I wanted to be in that.

Q. THE WHITE REVIEW — Do you feel the spoken word has always been the driving agent behind your work, that you have always been sound-led? I know you did a John Wieners project at Harvard in April on the poetic applications of the Boston sound.

A. EILEEN MYLES — I think encountering O'Hara was like permission; if that's what he sounded like, I was about finding out what I sound like or what this sounds like, this conversation, anything – and trying to figure out how to use that. I had gone to graduate school very briefly and taken a linguistics class, where there was so much talk about black English. I was just starting to realise that language is multiple, and that whatever English I speak is both acquired and received. There were people from many different classes in my neighbourhood when I was growing up, and then arriving in New York meant encountering a whole other variety, so it has always been a cobbling together of sounds. The guy I'm reading with tonight, Fred Moten, is a scholar and a black American who writes in

a vernacular too, and I think that our avant-gardism is really a pastiche of different kinds of speech. Even the O'Hara thing, that kind of unitary self, is less what all of us are doing and more like a piece of what we're doing.

Q. THE WHITE REVIEW — I was struck by how different the experience of hearing you read your own poetry was in comparison to reading it on the page. As someone who experiments with the idea of the self as a performance, how did it feel to see someone else perform you on TRANSPARENT?

A. EILEEN MYLES — I feel like I'm the perfect poet to have that experience because I grew up in the fifties and the sixties as a kid with early television, which was right out of radio and vaudeville, and it was kind of this moving smorgasbord, nobody knew what it was yet. So many shows started with someone sitting down with their chin on their hand telling you what you're about to hear, sort of like Hitchcock, there was just like an emceeing of culture, and I feel like in my poems I'm doing that emceeing. And so it's so funny to look at TRANSPARENT and see me being emceed. I feel what's fun is that this character who is not me but is me could potentially be introducing people to poetry, and I love that.

Q. THE WHITE REVIEW — How does one navigate that space, of being at the centre of one's work but not making it about oneself? I remember you recently mentioning Frederick Seidel as a negative example of this.

A. EILEEN MYLES — Well, we always do that. We use what touches us, our times, our environment, and we show an actor, ourselves, moving through that space. If you write with a desire to use someone very much like yourself but not yourself, you show how every self is a chameleon. The most recent problem with Seidel is why did THE PARIS REVIEW choose to have his poem published in response to Ferguson? That was a great time to publish an astonishing, complicated poem by a black poet. It felt like this spot requires this form of address not that form of address, and the thing that was so strange was that THE PARIS REVIEW didn't seem to understand that. Instead, people felt like we had a white newscaster, Seidel, give a few thoughts. Wow. Yawn. Why? At this moment, we don't need to hear another white guy's speech.

Q. THE WHITE REVIEW —— I've been thinking about your writing on James Schuyler as well as your infamous Robert Lowell poem. Have you felt it a necessity to extinguish certain male idols, to de–mythologise one's work in a way?

A. EILEEN MYLES —— Well, Schuyler and Lowell are two different things. Schuyler is a great poet. No one cares about Robert Lowell any more. I wrote about Lowell in the mid-seventies, when I really was seeing the brouhaha about a poet dying for the first time. It was so corny. Let him go!

Q. THE WHITE REVIEW —— You wrote about Maggie Nelson and Dana Ward that 'part of the method of their madness is security', which struck me as something very telling about your own writing. There is a very strong sense of both vulnerability and certainty, of confidence and chance.

A. EILEEN MYLES —— One thing that's so great is that it's art, not life. And so if you're going to be sure someplace, why not do it in art? It's sort of like an amulet. Art is mythic, whereas this [gestures around the room] isn't, you know? Though it seems that this is the source. When I moved to New York at 24 I felt I had grown up with all my ambitions and desires – what am I

going to do and who am I going to be. And so the first realisation was that I'm going to be a poet: that's what I'm going to do. And that was a huge relief – there were so many things that I didn't have to worry about any more. I'd travelled a bunch when I was younger and it just didn't take. I'd go to San Francisco and then I'd go back to Boston, or I went to Europe and hitchhiked around for six months and then it was groan, go back to Boston. And finally going back to Boston that last time made me realise that I had truly left. After that, going to New York was like the afterlife. Once I was done leaving, I had to start going. So I went to New York and like it or not, I was at the end of the line and I had to begin. When I first got there, I remember having this dream, one of those dreams where you were awake in your dream, realising you were dreaming. And I remember thinking that about my life, that if this is a dream, let me be brave in it. I feel like that's never changed.

Q. THE WHITE REVIEW —— Of course I can't help but ask about your stance on the Hillary Clinton nomination.

A. EILEEN MYLES —— I knew we were both on that question before we even got to it.

Q. THE WHITE REVIEW —— I read your piece on BuzzFeed but then I remember you tweeting that your vote is shaken after her AIPAC speech, which was, well, pretty definitive. I know that absolute endorsements are fictions but: what do you think now?

A. EILEEN MYLES —— I think she has been blamed for being a woman who has had to decide at various points. Not all her decisions or my decisions are good decisions. It reminds me of something that James Schuyler once said. There's a story about him where they're looking at a painting and then somebody goes,

'It's the wrong pink', and he turns to them and says, 'Did you have some other pink in mind?' With Hillary, they're always saying, 'I'm for a woman being president but she's the wrong woman.' She is the woman we have right now. She is the only viable candidate. Of these three people that America has given us to choose from, she's the only one who actually could do it. Bernie is kind of a joke even when what he says is true or important – for me he just doesn't say it so well, and I'm kind of stunned that people have been so excited about the performance.

Part of it is that I know that it's a performance. I ran for president. I know what it's like to make speeches and to be thrilled by people. I'm a performer, I know what it's like to be thrilled by standing in a room and feeling the room be affected by you and feeling the room cheer for you, and it's great. Who wants to let go of that? But I keep having to say the same thing again: he's going to walk into Congress and say, 'Break up the banks,' and they're not going to do anything. It's just like, stop playing to the peanut gallery. I think he never stopped.

Q THE WHITE REVIEW — What about the accusation of 'corporate feminism', which arguably wouldn't lead to structural change?
A EILEEN MYLES — I think that 93 per cent of the time Bernie Sanders and Hillary Clinton voted the same in Congress, and that 7 per cent isn't necessarily about leftie things that he did. Some of that 7 per cent is him supporting the gun lobby and so tell me about her corporate feminism, and tell me about his. Whatever you want to call it, I like the thing that wants gun laws and I don't like the thing that doesn't. Also, Hillary did go to Palestine and she got so much shit for it, but she went. Of course, she changed her tune after that, but the fact that

she went meant that she felt something different at that time, and I feel like she could feel that again if she had power.

Q THE WHITE REVIEW — I am curious about your own presidential campaign. When did you decide to do it? It wasn't a performative gesture.
A EILEEN MYLES — It came from a very passionate place, from feeling that people like me were not represented in the campaign or the government or the future or America. Also at that time I had been doing work that was improvisational, performance pieces and speeches and talking and wanting to be more politicised, and then I suddenly realised that it was an election year, there was a campaign going on, and if I entered it as a candidate, I could talk about the things that I cared about and alter the campaign. Which to some extent I'm sure I did. How exactly I'll never know, but it was an amazing opportunity because what it produced was me becoming a repository of information for a lot of people. It was before the internet and so people were just giving me pamphlets, people would take me places, people would invite me places and show me things. It changed my perspective on what the situation in America was and what mattered. One of the things that's funny about right now is that if my life resembles any other period of time in my own past, it's when I ran for president, when suddenly I was bigger than my own boundaries and I had to figure out how to be there.

Q THE WHITE REVIEW — Do you think the wider recognition of the likes of Chris Kraus, Kathy Acker and Maggie Nelson signals a new cultural moment?
A EILEEN MYLES — We have begun to colonise the mainstream. At a certain point things

reverse and it stops being about people colonising us and we start to colonise you. Part of it is that the media is this way now. I think we need new forms of literature that acknowledge that free-flowing sphere of knowledge and sexuality. Art has to finally be the place where something gives and the form is forever different. I think the people you've mentioned – and my work too – describe this new world that we're living in now, where this isn't discrete anymore.

Q. THE WHITE REVIEW —— Who interests you right now in terms of other writers?

A. EILEEN MYLES —— What Maggie Nelson's doing is really exciting. Also Chris Kraus. Laurie Weeks. R. Erica Doyle. She has a book from Belladonna called PROXY. C. A. Conrad, who wrote THE BOOK OF FRANK, his work is really important to me. Then there's also Ariana Reines, of course. Dodie Bellamy. Kevin Killian. The first people who come to mind are people who are beginning to be known, who no-one knew last year. And then some of the people I'm excited about aren't even alive anymore, you know, like Bruno Schulz.

Q. THE WHITE REVIEW —— Do you have a preferred writing ritual or method?

A. EILEEN MYLES —— I like legal pads a lot. If I'm at home, I'll write on a legal pad. If I was anywhere, I would just grab a piece of paper. But mostly, if I was on a train, I would write in a diary. The thing I like about writing on paper as opposed to writing on the computer is that you're in the room. That seems so important. When you're on the computer, you're in the computer, sort of. I love Instagram, I love taking pictures, but when I'm in my notebook, I'm actually *on* the train, you know? I'm in my body and I feel like I'm even learning

something, though I don't know what it is that I'm learning. It reminds me of being a child. There was something about the burden of time and space when I was young that was so overwhelming and made me so twitchy that I just kept drawing.

Q. THE WHITE REVIEW —— What about form? There is a line in COOL FOR YOU where you say that the form of the novel gives dignity to shame.

A. EILEEN MYLES —— Yes, and I'm definitely thinking that that's a impulse that unifies many of the writers I care about. You start with a sense of abjection in living, either because of your caste or because of your lived experience. Then you write yourself out of that space, by giving it form.

Q. THE WHITE REVIEW —— What do you feel about this gendered discourse of intent that somehow interprets first-person confessional writing as 'secreted', 'flowing out', not written, revised, thought about?

A. EILEEN MYLES —— I would say secreted or leaked or splashed or barfed out, except that as it gets out the distance from here to there is aestheticised and filtered. I think about John Ashbery talking about poetry; he describes it less as a transcription of the thoughts you're having all day long, less as an experience than the experience of experience. I don't know why, I always find this really difficult to say — managed chance. You learn the art of management through a million small poems and assignments and performances and stuff, and then the larger question of your own existence comes up in big gulps and you have the chops. I think about these writers who we're talking about or other writers I might care about, and I think it's about bringing small skills to large endeavours. It's not MOBY DICK, it's *I LOVE DICK*, you know? This is not history, it's something else. I think poverty. I think purity. It bumps against pornography. There's no right name for it. But in a way it is more of a craft than a calling. And it's homely, in all the ways of using that word. Domestic.

^{Q.} THE WHITE REVIEW —— Do you feel the increased visibility of feminine abjection, in literature, television etc., is part of that?
^{A.} EILEEN MYLES —— Humans are abject. We are. I think it might be about the humanising of women. We are entering the species through the media and books. It's shocking that it took so long, but we had men writing for us so we didn't get to speak until recently. Earlier feminism required women to win and be superheroes. Our right to be losers has come slow.

^{Q.} THE WHITE REVIEW —— I remember last time we spoke you mentioned you are working on a new novel. A dog memoir?
^{A.} EILEEN MYLES —— Yes. It's finished and now at the editing stage. I'm calling it memoir and the funny part is that it's actually quite fictional, probably more than any other book I've ever written. It starts with an account of a dog dying. I had a very strong sense, when I looked into her eyes, that this was my father. My father died when I was 11 and we were very close, and when I got the dog I thought, 'Wouldn't it be funny if my father came back as my dog?' He totally would do that. He would want to be with me a little longer and I would want him to be with me a little more. And so I ran with that as a prompt. There's also a book called *ALL MY LOVES* and I think the idea is to just swoop in on moments in various kinds of love relationships, bits and pieces of them, and let that be one long book.

^{Q.} THE WHITE REVIEW —— May I ask what your tattoo says?
^{A.} EILEEN MYLES —— This is 'poeta che mi guidi', which is from the second canto in the *INFERNO*. It's when Dante met Virgil and he basically wanted to know if he would be able to walk through hell, and so he said, 'Poet, take my measure', you know, 'I think I can do it.'

MARIA DIMITROVA, JUNE 2016

TAKE CARE OF ME FOREVER

BY

JEN GEORGE

ON A BED IN THE EMERGENCY ROOM, being pumped full of morphine and oxycodone, vomiting, then being pumped full of the same medications, I recall the ways I've always been. I've always been afraid of not getting what I want. I've been that way since I was 4. I've always wondered why people look senseless in crowds when they fear a greater managerial organisation is not looking after them. I've been that way since I was in a crowd just recently. I've always had stomach pains and trouble with regularity. I've been that way since I was 5. I've always imagined how living people will look burning in the National Cremation Oven all people burn in when they die. I've always prayed in bed at night to something unknown, possibly the sky, as my ambitions were never excessively lofty. I've always thought I was destined for great things such as people taking pictures of me. I've always noticed how people appear to be excelling when doing basic life things like jobs or talking about articles. I've always wanted to be all things to all people. I've been that way since I was 8 and my doctor told me to give him a call when I was 18. I called him when I was 18. I said, 'Was there something you wanted to tell me?' The doctor said he'd have to retrieve my file and call me back. Several weeks later he called me back. 'You were a charming girl,' he told me. 'So flirtatious, overtly sexual. I'd like to marry you.' 'I'll have to think about it,' I told him. My mother said marry him – the money, the status, the savings on medical bills. I left a message with his secretary accepting the proposal, but by the time he got my message he had married another former patient who had also recently turned 18. My mother had already bought me a wedding dress. The dress became my favourite thing to wear most days, though my mother hated to see me ruin it through use.

A nurse approaches my ER bed, which I should not call mine because it is so temporary. 'You are dying,' she says.

My life was never almost something, which is possibly better than almost being something where dying is concerned. Once I rode a carousel and sat upon the white horse with a golden saddle. Another time I got drunk at the beach during the night and came across a party lit by tiki torches and paper lanterns where I had free champagne and cake. I skinny-dipped with strangers in the ocean then. It was a fantasy come to life. Once I fell deeply in love with a man I'd met only once. I'm not sure if he loved me, but I'd like to think he was fond of me. We'd had a nice conversation at a party and were very kind to each other. We smiled at one another throughout the evening. It is something to have such genuine, mutual feelings of kindness upon meeting someone. I had never before experienced it and have not since. After we parted ways, I thought of him. At night, I'd go to bed early so that I could lie in the dark and think of him. I'd imagine kissing him in the cafeteria at the Met, running into him on the street and getting a hotel for the afternoon, giving him a hand-job in his car during his lunch break while parked on the street. In each scenario we'd mostly masturbate one another or make love in the driver's seat or smile at each other, full of kindness.

After nearly two weeks in the ER, I receive a room in the hospital; it's actually half a room, partitioned by a curtain, next to the floor bathroom, with a small window next to the bed that looks onto a brown brick wall. The wall on my side of the curtain has a large crack that looks to be the result of a powerful earthquake or something rather large hitting the building. A woman behind the curtain on the other half of the room moans. A television plays a local channel currently airing old interviews of great people discussing subjects and opinions. An older woman in a yellow caftan, draped in beads, and with a ring on every finger, says, 'Life was never trouble for me. I just don't understand why people are always at odds with the world around them.' She is very beautiful. Titles under her image show that she is a great woman at philanthropy and organised events. 'One must be honest with oneself; this is a cardinal rule for harmony,' she says. A nurse comes and hooks me up to an IV. She gives me several shots in the back of my arm, takes a small hammer, like one made for breaking up brittles or toffee, from her pocket, hits the crack in the wall, and then leaves. Mice skitter in and out of the crack in the wall. I am left alone in the room, in my hospital bed, for several days. No one comes. The roommate moans.

Meal service begins after some time. A short man with a cauliflower ear appears to deliver my breakfast every morning. He cooks the food himself in the hospital kitchen. He puts hot sauce all over the scrambled eggs, the white toast, and the fresh mango so that I'm unable to eat it.

The discord amongst the nursing staff is apparent and often difficult to ignore. The night shift fights most loudly, but there is tension on all shifts. Sometimes they threaten to beat one another to a pulp. Other times they ask one another if they'd like to take this outside. They accuse one another of flat tyres, stolen mail, malicious spells preventing good fortune, adulterous relationships, spit in food, banana peels conveniently left in hallways, smelling bad, talking shit, being full of shit, shitting in the employee toilet without flushing. They talk about patients: about which ones are particular burdens, about which ones are sexy, about which ones are assholes, dipshits. One of the night nurses uses my bedside radiator to dry her pantyhose and underwear after she's washed them in the floor's bathroom sink. Another one watches me while I pretend to sleep.

After holding my bladder for several days, I decide to use the floor's bathroom for the

F

first time. In the bathroom, I notice a large hole in the wall. An opening. I enter the opening with my mobile IV. I make my way through pipes, drywall, and rotten wood into what seems to be a strip mall dentist's office hallway. All of the office doors are locked and the snack vending machine at the hallway's end is empty. The janitor's closet is the only open door. Inside there is a mop and a toilet plunger covered in dried toilet paper next to a small bucket of teeth. There's an opening partially covered by a poster of a model in a crotchless dashiki. This opening leads outside, to the exterior of the hospital, which shares its wall with a football stadium. The stadium lights are on. I walk onto the football field and, as I approach its centre, I recognise several things: a collection of VHS tapes on a bookcase, a TV/VHS set playing VAN GOGH AND GAUGUIN: A LOVE STORY, and a stool upon which sits a naked painter with a very small penis. I recognise the painter as someone I used to do sex games with, only I didn't know they were sex games at the time. The things surrounding him are his belongings from his old bedroom. I sit upon the grass below the stool in the middle of the football field. The painter holds a brush in one hand, a palette in the other. He's painted a poorly mixed ochre/burnt sienna beard on his face with oils. The painter looks as though he's exhausted himself with attempts at important work.

'Cry for my little penis, you stupid fucking bitch,' he says, maybe playing one of our old sex games. He continues to work on a scene of himself in a matador's costume with a crown of marigolds atop his head, several slayed bulls at his feet. I cry for the painter's little penis. I've been told I could have been a professional mourner had we lived in a society that allowed mourning. I wink at the small penis as I cry, letting it know we are playing a game.

'Do not tease me,' the painter says.

'This is no tease,' I tell him.

'I remember you,' the painter says. 'I have loved great women: French women, Mexican women, blonde women, spiritualist women. You can get lost in a spiritualist pussy for hours. You were not one of the greats partly because your looks are average, but primarily because you did not bed other great artists – painters or writers or sculptors or anyone great. That may have affected my ability to become a great artist myself.'

'I'm sorry,' I say. 'Did you ever have babies? When we were lovers you painted ghost babies in carriages.'

'No, I did not,' he says. 'The great love of my life with whom I wanted to have children left me because of the penis.'

'I still have a scar from where you burned me with a cigarette,' I tell him. I show him the scar beneath my armpit. 'This is lasting and I cherish it, though I quit smoking some time ago because of the Surgeon General's warning and an accidental wildfire. I don't recall what your penis felt like inside of me. You went down on me a few times,

F

but only in the early hours of the morning and only when I wore white cotton underwear. We drank opium tea together. You said you did not want to corrupt me.'

'You were so dumb,' he says. 'Your pubic hair had not come in at 22 years of age. Your nipples were the most nascent pink; I've never been able to recreate the right colour with my paint. Now I am confined to this chair because I was consumed by thoughts of fucking when I was supposed to be a devout Buddhist. I had taken certain tantric vows that I reaffirmed and broke daily over a six-year period. It turns out there's a price to pay – I'll remain on this stool for twice that length as punishment.'

'I'm dying,' I tell him. The painter continues to paint.

'If you want me to paint your deathbed scene, I'm afraid that ship has sailed. After that artist from Chino got famous for his deathbed scenes, it kind of ruined it for me.'

'Do you watch these tapes to pass the time?' I ask.

'The only one that works is *VG & G: A LOVE STORY*. Luckily it's my favourite film. The scene where Gauguin and the ghost of Van Gogh have a threesome with the 14-year-old Tahitian girl is my favourite part.'

'We watched this once, together,' I tell him. I stroke his oil-paint beard. 'You looked in the mirror behind the television as we watched. You painted your self-portrait while you masturbated onto my asshole.'

'That very portrait hangs in my gallery. I captured my image at the moment of ejaculation perfectly. The gesture is a great artistic accomplishment. My own image is all I paint now.'

Upon the field, near the field goal, there is a small three-walled, roofless gallery in which dozens of self-portraits of the painter are hung. All of them are in his style, none of them great. My IV bag has emptied of fluid and has started to draw blood into the bag. The painter tells me he must get back to work.

I say goodbye to the painter and return to the hospital through the empty strip mall dentist offices. Back in my half room, the roommate moans.

I have always been an insomniac and in this place there is much to think about in the early hours of the morning. I think of the ways I am trying to become a more self-aware or fully realised person, for harmony. If I am honest with myself, there was always a limit to my potential. If I am honest with myself, any man will fuck you if you let him masturbate onto your asshole. If I am honest with myself, I don't know what I did with all or any of my days. If I am honest with myself, it is a relief. Angel food cake is my favourite food. Nothing was as good as I'd wanted it to be. I have always had an adulterous mind and as a result would not make a good wife. I prefer the missionary position but only in cases where the man is much, much larger than myself, more like a giant than obese, and smothers me to a point where I cannot breathe and begin to lose consciousness. If I am honest with myself, I only think about

F

sex for the fantasy of attention or obliteration rather than pleasure.

Over the next week I am wheeled about the hospital. Early one morning, before sunrise, I am wheeled into the MRI room and lifted onto the bed of the machine. The operator talks to me through the speaker.

'Just relax,' he says.

'I am relaxed,' I say.

'Relax further,' he says.

'How?' I ask.

'Breathing.'

'I am breathing.'

'Kegels,' he says. I do some kegels.

'I'm done,' I say.

'More,' he says.

I only pretend to do more.

The operator plays Béla Bartók through the speakers. 'This will take quite a while,' he says. But all things here take quite a while.

On a rainy day I'm brought to a room marked Gynaecological Exploration and laid on a flat table, then strapped down. The table is adjusted with a crank to a 90-degree angle so that my pelvis and legs are raised. 'Hydrosonogram,' a doctor tells the room full of students. My hospital gown is lifted to my breasts and forceps are inserted into my vagina. 'Vaginal probe,' the doctor says. I feel a cold metal rod enter me. 'Come have a look,' the doctor tells the students. The students approach wearing headband flashlights. 'An unusual vaginal cavity,' someone says. 'Crystal-like stalactites,' says someone else. 'Curious,' I hear someone say. 'This is my first uterine cavity,' a voice, somewhat excited, comments. 'This is my favourite uterine cavity,' says another. A catheter is placed up my uterus and then I feel a balloon-like apparatus being inflated. 'More solution,' the doctor says. The balloon gets larger. I feel my uterus may explode. 'My uterus is going to explode, or is it my cervix?' I say. The crowd laughs. After I am lowered and unstrapped, my hospital gown placed in its original position just below my crotch, the students shake my hand. One slips me his number. Another has a visible erection through his coat while he pulls diaper-like underwear over my pelvis. 'Heavy bleeding may occur,' he tells me. I can't be sure, but I think I've been here, in the hospital, at least a few weeks. I think of my cat, of my apartment, for which I do not have this month's rent. Maybe I can make a credit card payment to my landlord over the phone in case they find a diagnosis, antidote, or cure for my condition. Maybe my cat has found a new home.

Following a seventeenth X-ray in as many days I am placed in an armless body cast in the room marked Casting, Mummification & Other. The doctors, having looked over all of my previous X–rays and test results, think it's the best thing. 'We can't be certain, but all of your bones are broken,' a doctor tells me. 'Had any falls down large staircases or out of windows of tall buildings? Maybe hit by a truck? Brutally beaten with a cast iron pan or a brick?' The casting takes twenty–four hours during which time I watch the local channel's OLD INTERVIEWS WITH GREAT LOCALS marathon. A woman in a light pink cape, hair done in a large bun that resembles a mushroom cap, who excels at beginnings though she is great at all points in a process, speaks to a host. 'Begin in time,' she says. 'The place to start is always clearly defined by a first action.'

In the Psychiatry & Other wing I'm wheeled into a large room with heavy orange carpets and brown furniture. The attendant locks the brakes on my bed. An egg–shaped, balding man with a large beard and a high–pitched voice sits behind a desk writing notes in a ledger. 'Your history,' he says.

'Yes,' I say.

'A depressive personality, fear of open spaces, unprovoked crying spells, extreme self–doubt, and a nervous heart, as evidenced by your recent test results.'

'Yes,' I say.

'Was your mother this way?'

'She was, though I've never been as bad as her.'

'Your condition could be entirely psychosomatic,' he informs me, 'much like your mother's fear of dying on an operating table.'

'She did die on an operating table,' I tell him.

'According to the records, she told everyone in the hospital she was going to die on that table. It was labelled suicide by self–fulfilling prophecy.'

'My mother committed suicide?'

'We feel you may as well. I subscribe to the notion that the apple doesn't fall far from the tree, primarily where flaws are concerned.'

'I'd like to know your lifetime accident and mishap history,' a new doctor says while sitting upon my bed. He has a tape recorder and microphone with him to interview terminal cases regarding lifetime accidents and mishaps for an art film he's making using patients as subjects. He tells me he gets actors to re–enact the histories of patients, films them, then projects all the films at once, each story crossing over onto other screens and stories, culminating 'in a symbolic and actual orgy between all charac–ters/patients/actors'. The artist/doctor says his project, titled THE WORLD AS WILL AND REPRESENTATION AND THE DESIRE FOR PENETRATION, stems from his observa–tion that all of life is the pursuit of wish fulfilment and wish fulfilment is inherently always sexual in nature. 'Genesis of the accident or mishap stems from thwarted wish fulfilment as a result of our Puritanical lineage,' he tells me. 'The accident or mishap operates as a valid event or precursor for the action of ill fortune in hopes we may end our suffering and inability to achieve fulfilment through events following the accident – embarrassment, illness, death – rather than allow our desires to surface or act upon them.' I am incredibly flattered an artistic and medical person would want to use me for his film. The artist/doctor tells me he's an artist over a doctor and that there are so few artists who are actual doctors it makes him unique amongst his contemporaries. 'I refuse to limit myself; self-censure through limitation in both action and imagination due to societal rules, expectations, or familial upbringing is the direct cause of the tragedy of the individual,' he says.

Because of my condition, I've been assigned a religious counsellor. 'I'm here to offer you the assistance you may need to make peace before your time comes,' the religious counsellor says.

'Once, my friend and I made a girl with cerebral palsy drink a concoction of coke, spit, and fire sauce,' I tell him. I have always liked the idea of confession. I'd like to be forgiven.

'I'm not a priest,' he says.

'Another time, with some neighbourhood kids, we made an older boy with Down's bike over broken glass on his training wheel bike. It popped his tyres and he cried. Everyone laughed. I pretended to laugh so no one could tell I was crying. But maybe everyone was crying.'

'I'm more accustomed to general conversation topics like "What happens to the soul?" – to which I answer things like "What do you think?" And then I sit and listen or give that impression.'

'What do you think happens?' I ask. My mother taught me to be accommodating to everyone at all times, but especially to people with roles and titles. The religious counsellor walks to the window and stares out at the brick wall.

'I think there's extreme fear and then nothing,' he says. 'Blackness. Out like a light.'

'So make it count?' I say.

'There is a lot of pressure to do things,' he says. 'What did you do with your life before your illness?'

'Nothing,' I say.

The religious counsellor clears his throat and stands next to the window looking onto the brick wall. 'You are not given much time,' he says, his back to me, his tone taking on a stage quality. 'And then you realise things too late, of course, and the time that remains is not enough time to actively change anything, to build anything, to do anything differently, better.' He turns toward me and looks into the near distance, his eyes not quite focused on the curtained partition. 'You are left with the knowledge

F

that things could have been done differently, better. There was no need to panic. Or worry. Or manipulate. Or despair. You could have tried. You could have worked hard. But mostly you could have done things differently, better,' the counsellor says. He looks at me, smiling. 'How was that delivery?' he asks, his voice returning to normal. 'Those are the lines in a local play I'm auditioning for.' 'Very convincing,' I say. I think he will get the part. 'Do me a favour and fill this out.' He leaves a survey atop my body cast. The first question asks, *Did our Religious Counsel leave you with a sense of comfort and security as regards your passing?* On a scale of one to five, five being 'strong sense' and one being 'no sense at all', I check five. Out like a light.

I must be bathed so I am removed from my body cast in the Sanitation wing. My body is shrivelled and weak. My ribs, protruding, and my wrists, so thin, are somewhat beautiful. The nurse informs me I've been diagnosed with auto–pregnancy, which she says has nothing to do with the fact that I'm dying. My uterus stores sperm then fertilises an egg every month. 'Like an internal sperm bank,' the nurse tells me. She explains that there is sperm inside me from every man I've ever slept with so the father of the potential foetus could be any one of them at any given time. The nurse informs me that I miscarry early on each pregnancy. 'Maybe that's why I feel a great sense of loss at all times,' I say to the nurse. 'Maybe,' she says. When I'm put back in the body cast I paint babies in the likeness of all the different men I've slept with upon my chest, stomach, and thighs. The night nurse, with a cherub print on her scrub shirt, enters my curtain while I paint with my nightlight on. 'How cute!' she says. I tell her I am painting my sons. Over the hospital's loudspeakers they play the recording of a hurricane that's recently been released as an album and is number one on the charts. Static. Wind. No voices.

On the local news it shows my neighbourhood, destroyed by the hurricane. People sit on top of crumbled buildings playing music from solar-powered radios and eating bagged lunches that have been dropped from helicopters. The camera pans by what looks to be the remains of my old building. It has burned to the ground. A newscaster interviews a neighbour who told me, one day when I was returning home from the grocery store, that he'd like to wiggle his thumb around in my ass. The reporter asks my neighbour about the content and quality of the bagged lunches provided by the Nation. 'Baloney sandwich. Peanut-butter crackers, the orange kind. A Jell-O cup, blue. It's pretty good.' My neighbour gives a thumbs-up, wiggles it.

My newest diagnosis from the psychiatrist is prolonged sexual fantasy. He gives me a sustained wink and then unzips the long crotch of his polyester pants, keeping his penis below the desk. He masturbates in his leather chair then comes onto a little

F

rubber asshole he grabs from the top of the desk. When he is finished I am wheeled back to my room.

The artist/doctor comes to visit me. He comes to visit me often now. He brings me new paints and brushes for my body cast in order to encourage my attempts at creativity. He looks over my chart and makes a few notes in his art notebook. He'd like me to elaborate on one of the accident and mishap recordings he's been listening to with the actresses, about the time I split a fellow student's lip in an outburst of anger after I'd found him eating candy from my backpack. It was an accident because I'd not intended to split the boy's lip. He'd had to get stitches. The artist/doctor wants to know more about the moment when I'd decided upon violence, so the actresses might better understand the scene.

'Were you angry?' he asks. The artist/doctor pats the hairs that stick out from the hard cast covering my head.

'I suppose I was. But mostly I think it was sugar addiction.' 'You loved sweets,' he says. 'You were afraid of not having candy.' 'It would've been easy to buy more. Fifty cents.'

The artist/doctor brushes the breasts of my cast. It is somewhat loving.

At my weekly appointment in the Psychiatry & Other wing, inside the orange and brown room, my psychiatrist asks for the details of my bowel movements. When I tell him I've only been able to urinate in a bedpan due to my body cast and subsequent limited mobility, and therefore have been unable to take note of my bowel movements, he suggests the Sleeping Room for reprogramming to achieve active bowel movements. He informs me that the heavy sleep state is induced through extremely high dose intravenous narcotic drugs. 'While the patient sleeps, recordings of my voice play on a small tape recorder under the patient's pillow. When it's all over, you'll be more self-reliant and have properly shaped stools.'

'I haven't been eating,' I tell him, mostly because I am hungry. 'The hot sauce burns my mouth and throat.'

'I hadn't guessed an eating disorder, but it's quite clear now that anorexia can be added to your diagnosis. And bulimia, going by your rotting teeth. There's no telling how wasted away you are under that cast. We'll reprogramme you for that in the Sleeping Room, too. It should only take about ten days with both programmes.'

The artist/doctor comes to visit me before I'm to go to the Sleeping Room. I tell him I'm afraid of sleeping for ten days with the messages of the psychiatrist playing in my ears, that the psychiatrist's egg shape is unnatural. The artist/doctor rubs the legs of my cast. He offers to paint symbols on my cast to protect me from anything harmful.

F

'I've been dabbling in shamanism,' he says. 'I excel at everything I do and the shaman thing is proving to be no exception.' I am impressed. 'I have never excelled,' I say. He describes ridding a neighbour's home of her ex-stalker's spirit. 'The stalker was a former friend of my neighbour, a woman who had been breaking into her house and sitting on her couches, looking over her bills, reading her personal journals, and placing her genitals on various household items while my neighbour was at work. The stalker later committed suicide and made a point of haunting my neighbour. I made a powder of conch shell, lily of the valley, white sage smoke, and a guard dog's saliva, put it in all the windows, at the doors and then, at the stroke of midnight, read from journals of the stalker/haunter/deceased that I'd picked up at the estate sale in front of the stalker's house. I chose especially poorly written and embarrassing passages so as to shame her. At first it made the spirit violently angry; she smashed mirrors, threw electronics in the toilet. I then said a few incantations and she left, just like that. I banished her to a realm in which she will never stop ageing and never complete any work — she was a struggling playwright. Perhaps it was a cruel sentence. I've since become sexually involved with my neighbour, though I'm unsure about the ethical boundaries of shamanism. I assume it is like most things; rules are in place, but made to be ignored.' The artist/doctor/shaman uses gold paint from my palette to paint various circles, triangles, polygons, and cycles of the moon on my cast. He paints an eight-pointed star on my third eye. 'Strength,' he says. 'Infinity,' he says. 'All things are nothing but manifestations of being,' he says, spitting on my forehead. I look at his work on my cast with pleasure. I have always wanted to be protected.

I sleep for two hundred and forty hours, as prescribed, in the Sleeping Room. I'm unsure if I'm dreaming or if the Sleeping Room is in fact a place altogether different from the hospital. Either way, I am somewhere else, out of my body cast, but still unable to walk. In this place, the artist/doctor and I are married. He is my husband. I am his wife, but I am rather small. The symbols he painted on my cast are now tattoos over my face and body. He picks me up from our bed, which is in a room atop a large hotel in the mountains, and he carries me about the hotel like a child, showing me what things are. 'That is a table,' he says. 'Over there is a wall clock at which we look to tell time so that we may perform appropriate activities at their designated hour. There is a painted marble bust. There is a bust of your breasts; there is one in each room of the hotel. We eat breakfast at 7 a.m. I go horseback riding at 10 a.m.' He points out of the window at white horses on green grass surrounded by a white fence. Outside the fence, there is a forest of Mediterranean cypress trees. 'You are too little to come horseback riding,' he says. 'After lunch I do sculptures,' he tells me. He runs his fingers through my hair. 'Your name is Smyrna,' he says. 'Your name is Lyssa. Your name is Little Fool.' I watch the wall clock in the hotel for hours as the husband goes

F

about his actions. I make love with the husband in the mornings before breakfast and after his rides. He looks so elegant when dressed in his riding clothes. When we make love he keeps his long hair in a braid with a red ribbon tied in a bow at the bottom. He keeps on his riding cap and his blazer. He has his pants pulled down to the knee, just to his riding boots. Before he comes his mouth opens wide and he whips me with his crop on my rear end.

I have a nanny who watches the white horses through the window with me. Sometimes the horses jump the fence and run into the Mediterranean cypress forest. We can see them go for some time because of their whiteness against the dark greens and blacks of the forest. The psychiatrist's voice recordings come through the hotel's loudspeaker system, somewhat muffled. My nanny carries me on her back from room to room to comb my hair as the messages play through the hotel. 'Doing things,' the psychiatrist says. 'Personal satisfaction through autonomy.' 'Places reached on your own two feet.' 'Food for self-sufficiency and fertility.' 'We can have children together.' 'This is your psychiatrist speaking.' 'Suicide is for people who make bad decisions.' 'What I like cooked for me is as follows: roast beef, creamed corn, mac and cheese, potatoes au gratin, and spirit-infused desserts (rum cake, tiramisu, trifle).'

There are other guests at the hotel in the evenings. They sit in the dining hall and eat wild meats my husband has hunted in the forest. I sit at the children's/wives' table alone, as there are no other little wives and there are no children and I eat small cakes prepared by the hotel pastry chef. I recognise some of the guests: friends maybe, or people from the hospital. 'Where have you been?' they ask me, their mouths full of meat, their faces lit by the deep orange and yellow flames from the candles and oil lamps. My nanny asks them, 'Where have you been?' They'd all like to know where each other has been. No one knows. They cannot believe their eyes at seeing each other after long absences, during which time they forgot one another's existence. They did not expect to see each other at dinner in this hotel. My husband gives toasts, he tells people to enjoy the grounds and the beautiful wall clock and the busts of his wife's breasts in each room. This night he unveils a new sculpture that will live in the dining hall. '*PENIS WITH LEGS*,' he says. I recognise the penis as my husband's own. The hotel guests clap. 'Such talent,' they say. 'An appropriate name for that very sculp-ture.' My nanny kisses me on the ear. 'Where have you been?' she whispers.

The psychiatrist comes in over the loudspeakers. 'You will get a job; a person needs to keep busy.' 'Help Wanted: Seeking pleasant, pretty, "open" type to make cof-fee, listen to problems and musings of (all male) staff in engine building warehouse. Ordering lunch (sexy phone voice a must), flirtatious with all staff, most flirtatious/sexual/sexually available with boss. Hours 9–5 plus after-work bar trips to laugh at jokes of/go home with boss. Must not have boyfriend. Candidates with cute room-mates A+.'

F

Following the Sleeping Room, my newest diagnosis from the rotation staff is midterm pregnancy with a high risk of foetal abnormality (all kinds). 'Congratulations,' the genetic counsellor tells me. I get many congratulations from the hospital staff. 'You're so skinny,' a nurse says. 'Children are a blessing,' a woman in a wheelchair says. At my weekly appointment, my psychiatrist calls me a tease and punches his desk after reading my chart. 'I should kill you,' he says. A genetic counsellor orders an amniocentesis to determine the nature of the foetal abnormalities. In the Procedures room, nurses in training saw through the cast covering my stomach in order to expose the area so that they may perform the procedure. A needle is plunged through my concave stomach in search of the amniotic sac. I cannot see the screen showing the interior of my uterus, but I can feel the needle searching. Following the procedure, the genetic counsellor goes on vacation to Mexico for two weeks, after which he informs me that the amniocentesis found that my pregnancy was a ghost pregnancy. 'Turns out the chances of you being pregnant were 1 in 100,000,' he says. 'I have never been good at maths.' He hands me tissues though I am not crying. 'The Gulf is beautiful this time of year,' he says. 'There are enormous floating oil slicks covering large swathes of the bright blue water's surface from Mexico to Bermuda, which make for fantastical psychedelic rainbow patterns.' In my room I paint another son in the likeness of the artist/doctor over the newly plastered stomach of my cast.

The artist/doctor wheels me to an unmarked room in the Psychiatry & Other wing at the middle of which sits a car without an engine. It is a replica of his own car, he tells me, down to the scratches on the paint and pens and empty energy drink cans on the floor. He places me in the passenger seat and he sits in the driver's seat. The lights go down and images are projected onto the wall that make it look like we're in a bad neighbourhood parked next to a dumpster that's overflowing with trash. A trash scent is pumped through the room. I smile at him. He smiles at me. We are full of politeness. He turns the knobs on the radio, but no music comes. He unzips his pants. I reach over with my recently de-casted hand to rub his penis. I spit on his penis. I smile at the artist/doctor, spit dribbling down my chin. I lean over to give him head. He pulls my hair back. I stick two fingers up his asshole. I take his testicles into my mouth. I look up at him and see that he is jotting down notes in his art notebook and on my chart. I try to do better, flat tongue, good suction, zero teeth. He sighs heavily, as though taking a good shit. I pause. 'You are so productive,' I say. 'Don't stop,' he says. I begin again. His pubic hair smells strongly of antibacterial soap. Eyes closed, sighing, he holds his notebook in one hand and grips the steering wheel. The artist/doctor is not the man who was so kind, the one that I loved, but the kind one that I loved is all I can think of in the moment. I pause again. 'You are so kind,' I say, not to the artist/doctor but to the man who was so kind, the one I loved. 'Shhh,' the artist/

F

doctor says, 'shut up.' I begin. When the artist/doctor comes the volume is so great I cannot swallow all of it. I manage to get a good deal of it down before I vomit on the empty coffee cups in the drink holders. The artist/doctor writes me a prescription for a powerful anti–nausea medication typically reserved for terminal cancer patients on intensive chemo.

A group of actresses from the artist/doctor's film come to my half of the room to talk with me about my character, about accidents and mishaps and the feelings and events surrounding the incidents specifically. The young women wear wigs so that their hair looks like mine. They're in their early twenties, drink large cups of coffee, and wear black turtlenecks and short navy schoolgirl skirts like I did ten years ago. They want to know everything about my character. 'I think she is a complete fool, but brave in her stupidity,' one says. 'I think she is a violent suicidal narcissist sex addict who damages anyone close to her,' says another. 'I think she is a little rabbit,' a girl with her wig on lopsided says. 'The kind of rabbit I'd like to pet and keep in a cage and take out on the lawn sometimes. The kind of rabbit you'd have to watch closely because a coyote will snatch her up or she'll have a heart attack if she hears the garbage truck, but at the same time you kind of secretly hope that something like that happens.'

'Once I fell down the stairs in front of a large group of people at a party when I was just out of high school,' I say. They take notes. 'I hurt my rear end,' I continue. 'Quite badly.' They sip their coffee and study my movements as I speak. 'I was embarrassed that I fell,' I go on. 'So I asked my friend to drive me home immediately, but she was trying cocaine for the first time and wanted to stay.'

'Did you stay?' an actress asks. 'I did,' I say, 'though I was very sore. I did a lot of coke and tried to look at the stars for a long period of time in order to avoid social contact, but I became more embarrassed and my injury hurt worse – like it was serious. At one point in the evening I confided my injury to someone who seemed friendly and he responded with a shrug, then walked away. For the rest of the night, I pretended I wasn't hurt when people would pass me and say hello.' Looking at the actors surrounding my hospital bed, I feel wise for a moment. 'I think much of life is pretending you're not hurt,' I tell them. No one writes this information down. 'Like an animal or something,' I say. Their pens rest on their notebooks. 'To protect yourself,' I say. They check their wristwatches, the kind I used to wear to be old-fashioned.

The young women ask more questions about other little accidents and mishaps and sit with me for a couple of hours. They've all taken extensive notes, though none on the points I consider important. They all seem to care about the project they're working on. They love showing up to set, which I have yet to see. They talk about their admiration for the artist/doctor's work. They talk about the curve to his penis when it's hard, their favourite sex positions with him. They talk about their daily lives, about their artists' world, about how they found a warehouse building near the Fulton Mall and take up the entire top floor. They talk about who's having a show where and doing what and dating who. They have so many plans.

The nurse who sometimes watches me pretend to sleep sits by my bed. 'There will never be any progress,' she says. She takes the brittles and toffees hammer to the crack in the wall. Mice run around the room.

I receive with my breakfast a flier for a local play, SICKNESS UNTO DEATH & THE PROLIFERATION OF GARBAGE, that features several of the hospital staff, including the hospital religious counsellor and the expert I saw on the television programme QUESTIONS. A local laundromat owner is quoted on the flier saying, 'Anticipation amongst the locals is reaching fever-pitch. We're all hoping to have some nagging questions answered and see some of the self-proclaimed talent in the community deliver – we'll be the judge of their so-called gifts.' The play will be staged inside the hospital chapel.

The artist/doctor wheels me to the Recreational wing and saws through my body cast at my nipples, crotch, and asshole. The artist/doctor asks me to masturbate for him by pressing my thighs together. Right before I come, he penetrates me, preventing orgasm. 'I love you,' I say. 'Shhh,' he says. He takes notes in his art notebook as he fucks me. 'You have a tightass pussy,' he tells me. I wonder how my pussy differs from the actresses who play me. 'When you sleep with the actresses who play me does it feel the same?' I say. 'Shhh,' he says. 'Do we have the same tightass pussy?' I say. 'Yes,' he says, 'shut up.' I am relieved we all have the same tightass pussy. It makes me feel a part of something.

My latest diagnosis is extreme lethargy. The following week I receive a diagnosis of hyper-delusional thought patterns. The next week they tell me I have an interest in all the wrong things. I'm diagnosed with a collapsed lung filled with blood. Slow moving septic shock. A body-shaped/sized mucus plug. I'm told if I have even an accidental orgasm, in a dream or anywhere, it'll most likely be the straw that breaks the camel's back. I'm told to limit sexual activity due to active ruptures in the uterus. I am told I should've had children younger. I'm told I'd have been an unfit mother. I'm told my life made a clear line to this place, like predetermined destiny. I'm told there is a ghost rod in my ass that remains from situations in which I was uncomfortable as a child.

The man with the cauliflower ear who brought food no longer brings food. I do not feel hunger or weakness and like to think I am entering an enlightened meditative state in which I am sustained by only intravenous drugs.

F

It is winter. There are several inches of snow on the window ledge. A nurse comes in to tell me everyone in the hospital has gone. 'Winter holiday,' she says. The janitor still sweeps the halls and delivers tabloid magazines full of stories about locals stumbling out of bars like Hank's Local with people who are not their spouses, or at parties celebrating business openings. There is an interview with the painter from the football field discussing his sentence and the ways in which having time to think has changed his work. 'More me,' he says.

I await news of the premiere for *The World as Will and Representation and the Desire for Penetration*, which is supposed to screen following the New Year. I realise I do not know if the artist/doctor is highly regarded in artistic circles. Due to my fragile ego, I hope the film is favourably reviewed.

My drip has run dry but I think there is enough in me cumulatively that it does not matter. I should visit the painter to ask him about the usage of time and then plan things: a curtain for the window, a rug beneath my hospital bed, a door that locks for the floor bathroom, mucus plug extraction, a trip to the dentist's office in the strip mall for some long overdue root canals. But it is winter and I have no shoes.

I have visions of the artist/doctor: the actresses that play me, who are dressed as I was in my early twenties, surround him on set. He gives them notes. When the artist/doctor yells action, the actresses move about, stubbing their toes, dropping glasses, cutting their bangs too short, farting loudly in quiet public places, joining in a massive orgy in which they feel both free and left out. The artist/doctor yells cut, critiques them, tells them to give more or give less, and begins rolling again. He provides them with work. They are forever devoted to him for giving them this purpose.

YANYAN HUANG

TRUE COLOURS

BY

SAM RIVIERE

CONSCIOUS UNCOUPLING

I wear the same clothes every day

Because every day I feel basically the same

Just some plain robes will be fine

And good luck trying to get a signal on Mount Sinai in this weather

A friend registers an opportunity like a business

Offering limited access

But fuck that, I want the codes

The feeling of having a phone in each pocket

As I come down the hill with fresh updates

Sharing is totally passive aggressive

I really believe that

But I feel generous when smashing your fake tablets for the bronze fragments

Even if the pictures depress me

I can profit

When a business leaves you

My iPhone is a poetic device

Severing your contacts

And from the number its name

WHITE PIZZA

There comes a time when you stop even seeing McSweeney's emails

In a landscape littered with large carapaces

Interns are wading through the slush sustained only by bloody marys

Poetry doesn't make any sense

In a socialist utopia

But motherfucker this is Media City

And like a true bourgeois I love surveillance

In fact any aberrant behaviour consecrating the self

The least unique aspect of any person is their feelings

The interns agreed as I cancelled their contracts and bought the quesadillas

This was the era before the end of analysis

And the theory of success as the deferral of pleasure

When I felt the schwing of fascism

Laying hungry and happy in a glade of wildflowers

Perfectly friendless

Still recovering from my twenty-five second obsession with Teresa Oman

I experience an unexpected negation

Like a photographer at a permissible spectacle

When I find out she's Australian

TRUE COLOURS

Straight white males only do disaffected don't they

I mean what else is there

Just so you know I'm sipping on an effervescent drink

A similar blue–yellow

To the eerie evening light that's currently

Planging off the suburbs

Where a day–moon waits to field it

Behind that line of bone–dry beach towels

Looking cheesier than ever

Just gusting on its anthem

And a breeze inflates my shorts

As too late I work out all my problems

Stem from dressing like I had black hair

Like I could somehow pull off green

Next time I look the moon has flaked or faded

The urge to take a picture departing long before it

And in agreement the pages of the hardback notebook

That I dare not write in riffle

Blueish

Nothing about them but their privilege

MINDFULNESS

My friend had begun sending clips of blank walls overlaid with his maniacal
laughter

Not quite summer

And crying in the Starbucks

You were recording the May riots

With dispiriting results

And there were hopes for a late

Light period

Even if most were already living like doomed celebrities

Holed up in discrete buildings

On the verge of perpetrating acts of artistic barbarism

I perceived a spoon as the title of a plate of food

Sweated the legacy of my centre parting

But we were all ailing

In the pallor of the decade

Some said that the abstract could save us

They called it new which was funny

And gathered in strong winds outside the hilltop residence of the famous DJ

While the sun went down

And harpies swooped off into the night...

You didn't want to be held

As the marathon diverged around us

Like everyone you were grappling with the now overwhelming realisation

That our session had expired

I chasmed

Between ordering

Those recycled seconds of empty hilarity

And the baristas chorusing our names together

INTERNET OF THINGS

It isn't chivalry

But maybe I'll stop watching if they discover an actor with structure

That is, someone not directly descended from peasants and farmhands

Like housecats appealing for treats

They tailor their cries for the spectator

When sugarwork toughens on a midriff

Imagination is a commodity

In that the poor don't have any

Hence the film industry and the significance of not-acting

When illustrating how to interface

With malleable caramel bodies many of which are old or dead now

You could call it social control if it weren't so obviously necessary

It doesn't matter

The future is scheduled

Next Saturday

On the flat earth

She will be farmed

For endurance art

As sirens from reality are heard through velvet foliage

And soft thunder

When a sunbeam pricks its crosshairs in a thigh gap

Shot without a fish–eye lens –

Where is the curvature

THINK PIECE

Conspiracies are the only art form left

And the art world is the biggest conspiracy there is

Find me in the ninteenth century leaning on a cloud

Where three distinct styles in trousers are having what looks to be a conversation

But is actually a strangely expressive foam

The patrons hunger beyond allegorical concision

Towards a new disinterest

Which sells because it doesn't get any closer or more distant

The artist needs private wealth

Like the state needs secret police

Committed to presence like a banal tsunami

In a café at the Met a man pedantically devours a chocolate brownie

A woman with a preternaturally thin neck pours some blended juice

We all require nourishment

Huge bowls of salad for Spanish girls in leather jackets

Private wealth is the secret secret police

Only the artist knows the scary story that produced it

I stole a cup of coffee

Because meaning must be a conspiracy

And I have paid for the freedom to discover it

If you find my Moleskine the reward is

The only reason I go to galleries –

To check out the ignorance

DON'T GIVE UP
THE FIGHT

BY

OSAMA ALOMAR

(*tr.* OSAMA ALOMAR & C. J. COLLINS)

DON'T GIVE UP THE FIGHT

While cavorting in a field, the wild horse felt overjoyed to see a water hose flailing in all directions, water spraying from it fearsomely as the farmer tried in vain to grab hold of it. The horse shouted as loud as he could, encouraging the hose, 'Don't give up the fight!'

    The hose answered him enthusiastically, 'Right on my friend!'

THE EARTHQUAKE

The unemployed young man suffered a psychological earthquake of eight points on the Richter Scale. It almost completely destroyed the city in which he lived. The loss of human life was horrifying.

The authorities were astounded at this unprecedented disaster. They undertook to rebuild the buildings of the city in a different form, reinforcing them with materials resistant to human earthquakes. Unemployed young men began to be regarded with utmost seriousness and caution. Unemployment was eradicated within a short time.

F

THE SHADOW

A terrible shadow spread slowly over the heads of the people, hiding from them the rays of the sun. No one dared look up to see the reason, instead they bent their heads even more than before while the huge shadow crept ever faster. Finally their days turned into the longest of nights. Life came to a stop. Daily activities stumbled. Sadness and depression spread throughout the country. But still no one dared to think even for a second to raise his head.

Rumours began to marry crazily and beget huge numbers of sons of all shapes and colours. Some said it was punishment from God for the people's level of moral decline and their heedlessness of principles and values. Others said it was a swarm of locusts such as had never been seen in all of human history and that it might last for many months. Scientists maintained that the lunar eclipse and the solar eclipse had become intermeshed and that this had formed the persistent black night. Life remained in this stumbling and sluggish state. The foundations of the civilisation on which the country had risen were broken and it fell to the earth with a terrible, loud sound. This caused its neighbours great joy and delight in its misfortune. A swampy tide of myths and rumours covered the country. The people began to suffer from pains in their backs and necks.

Finally a courageous young man appeared who decided to raise his head to the sky, despite the warnings of his family and friends, so that he might know the nature of this terrible thing that had entirely destroyed his country and returned the mindset of its inhabitants – even that of the scientists – to a primitive state.

But his surprise was great when he discovered that this disaster consisted of an extremely long tongue! He set off running as fast as he could, searching for the root of the tongue so that he could know whose it was. He discovered that it belonged to the small, ugly gang leader who, with the help of his henchmen, had prepared a strategic plan for destroying and pillaging the country for hundreds of years to come.

WAR

After much hesitation, the Aliens decided to visit Earth. In response to their longstanding desire as well as the constant messages that the Earthlings had been sending them for years, they laid out a programme for a long and detailed study of human nature and behaviour and a study of the planet in all its aspects. Their highly advanced spacecrafts took off from their planet which was located in the farthest region of the universe. In record time they reached the edge of the solar system and began to monitor the Earth with their scientific instruments in most precise detail in order to send the data back to their planet. The first things their cameras detected were nuclear explosions and severed human limbs piled up everywhere and millions of refugees pouring out in all directions. Everything they photographed was killing, destruction, desolation, and tongues of fire. The leader of the space fleet sent a short message to his planet saying, 'We are unable to land on Earth because it is utterly consumed in a crushing civil war.'

F

HORSES

I rode the horse of hatred. He carried me into strange places, rugged and trackless, filthy and full of wild beasts and poisonous reptiles.

I rode the horse of loving-kindness. He took me to places that enchanted my mind with their wonder and their magic to the point where I felt the sap of paradise seep into me and spread through my arteries and my veins.

But when I rode the horse of objectivity I went through places that had a little of this and a little of that.

F

THE GOD OF VIRTUES

After years of hesitation, Satan decided to make his own Facebook page and also to start a website in order to promote his principles. The idea seemed completely strange and crazy to the members of his tribe. But he tried with great enthusiasm to convince them of the advantages of the plan, assuring them of its long-term success. As soon as the website and the Facebook page were online, Satan began to send out friend requests accompanied by flashy pronouncements about goodness and loving-kindness, tolerance and the brotherhood of humankind, the rejection of hatreds, the embrace of human rights, and the need to fight oppression. This promotional campaign had great success among the people. Satan's happiness was indescribable. To the surprise of his tribe, his friends were counted in the thousands, and, shortly thereafter, in the millions. His site became the most famous in the whole world on social media. The globe overflowed with demonstrations of support, loyalty, and admiration for Satan, waving banners soaked in the perfume of love for the champion of goodness, justice, tolerance, and equality. Humanity was fully convinced that, by the hand of Satan, the building of heaven had begun on earth.

As for the Angels of God, destructive doubt about their nature started to tear at them savagely. Little by little, fangs grew in their mouths and claws on their hands. Terrifying features formed on their faces. Embryos of evil began to pulse madly in their depths, longing to be born for humanity's destruction.

F

QUESTION MARK

On a very clear night as I lay on the roof of my house gazing at the stars, I noticed in the empty spaces between them question marks far more numerous than the stars themselves. After a few minutes I fell into a deep sleep.

The next morning I sat on the veranda drinking a cup of coffee. I looked out on the silent plains and the mountains wreathed with clouds like giants wrapped in mystery. I saw countless question marks...

After I finished my coffee I went inside to shave. I saw myself in the mirror, the biggest question mark an eye could see... I stepped back in terror... Since that day I have a great hatred for question marks.

F

THE NAME

Despite his best efforts, the Author's name began to slide down off the top of the book's cover where it had been printed. The Author's self confidence had died long ago, but his name was determined to hang on to the spot where it belonged with all its might. It dug its nails into the smooth cover as the sweat poured off it, but its body, which had become unbelievably heavy, pulled it stubbornly down. Every so often it glanced fearfully into the abyss below it where terrifying creatures snapped their jaws hungrily. Its tears mixed with its sweat. Its body grew emaciated and its nails broke off. Clinging to the bottom edge of the cover it peered up with diminishing eyesight at the high peak where it had once sat. A moment later it dropped into the pit and was crushed by thousands of feet walking this way and that in a frenzied haste. As for the book, years later it was hailed as an anonymous literary masterpiece.

F

VIII

INTERVIEW

WITH

LEE UFAN

LEE UFAN CAME TO PROMINEECE IN THE 1960s as one of the most important proponents of Mono-ha ('School of Things'), a group of artists in Japan that attempted to undo the representational hierarchies prevalent in Western European and North American art. Rather than placing the emphasis on expressiveness, an attempt was made by artists including Kishio Suga, Nobuo Sekine and Susumu Koshimizu to eclipse the personality of the artist through the process of making. The inherent properties of materials were barely altered, while the separation of the artwork from the world around it was undone through an emphasis on the relationships between things and their environment.

The Korean-born artist is sometimes compared to his near-contemporary, the American minimalist sculptor Richard Serra, because of his use of industrial steel plates, but the differences in their works' effects on the viewer are far more important that any formal similarities. With Serra the viewer is faced with a confrontational object, while in Lee Ufan's work the spectator's body becomes a thing among things, in a more openly democratic vision of art and its capacities. Such a view also belies the attempt to view Lee Ufan's art through an Orientalist lens, as if the work were the expression of a kind of Zen metaphysics. Instead it might be said to constitute an alternate, if repressed, modernity, one that allows for an encounter with the world that is relational, non-hierarchical, and always provisional.

The following interview took place in July at Château la Coste near Aix-en-Provence, France, on the occasion of Lee Ufan's exhibition at the vineyard. His manner was relaxed, and he spoke amiably and with good humour via his interpreter.

———

Q. THE WHITE REVIEW —— In a 1969 essay titled 'World and Structure', you described your desire to present 'the world as it is'. Could you explain this statement and relate it to what came to be known as Mono-ha, or School of Things?

A. LEE UFAN —— This citation owes its existence to Aristotle and so to Ancient Greece. But it is often misinterpreted because in reality it is difficult, perhaps impossible, to see the world as it is. What I wanted to say with these words was that art can place reality between parentheses and cast it in a different light. The notion of representing the world as it is, however, may be a contradiction in terms.

Mono-ha can easily be defined. The movement was created in reaction to certain tendencies in Modernism, especially the importance placed on the will of the artist and the related notion of the artist as creator. Against these dominant views, the artists associated with Mono-ha decided to limit their interventions as much as possible and to leave empty spaces in their works, so as to enliven both what was made and what was not made. It is the relationship between these two elements that is central to Mono-ha.

Q. THE WHITE REVIEW —— I can see how the notion of the author is dismantled or deconstructed in your work – few artworks could be more self-effacing – but could you nevertheless describe some of the strategies you employ?

A. LEE UFAN —— Every case is different. As you have seen, I often work with stones and steel plates. Stones form part of nature, and I find them on walks in the mountains. I then try to intervene as little as possible. I want the stones to be left in their natural state. The same can be said for the steel plates. My role is then to reassemble the two elements.

One of the main ideas behind Modernism is to place yourself ahead of things. For example, in the gardens at Versailles, where I recently held an exhibition, there are many shrubs and plants with their own properties. But the designers of these gardens did not care about these properties. They wanted squares so they got squares, they wanted circles so they got circles. In this way order was imposed on nature. That for me is Modernism.

We find the same principle at work in sculpture. There are artists who will take stones and shape them into the image they hold in their minds. The concept comes first. That is not my approach. I take the opposite view. I take a thing from nature and minimise my intervention. In the end what is important to me is the relationship between different elements and the experiences this relationship might provoke in the spectator. It is crucial that there is a dialogue. But what is perhaps most important is the presence of ambivalence. I exist in indecision. Because the relations played out between things make you hesitate. Modern thought says that you must be clear and that you must know what it is you want in advance. I completely disagree. For me ambivalence is a good thing. The human is not an extraordinary or perfect thing but is filled with problems, just as vegetables and animals are. I want to make art that allows these imperfections to show through.

Q. THE WHITE REVIEW —— Mono-ha is typically translated as 'School of Things'. The expression is interesting – 'things' have recently become the subject of much debate in both philosophy and critical theory – and I wonder how you would distinguish between a thing and an object, an art object say. Because for me things carry more potential than objects, which might be seen as reductions. They are also more material.

A. LEE UFAN —— The term 'Mono' in Japanese does not mean an object, which is a word towards which I feel critical. 'Mono' is a broader term that can designate a great number of things. It can refer to a stone found in the mountains, to an industrial steel plate, to electricity, to a tree. But it can also designate a state of mind, a form of awareness. Because 'Mono' is something that we do not fully understand, something people find mysterious. That is why it is important to emphasise that the term does not simply mean an object.

When objects are conceived by people they are created on the basis of a concept. In 'Mono' the concept is removed. To remove the concept from the thing lends that thing its mystery. This is a method I find interesting: to separate a thing from its concept. Whether an object is an art object or an everyday object is not a difference that interests me. What interests me is the object in its metaphysical state. When you have a stone in the middle of the mountains no one will look at it, no one will notice it. But when I take this stone and place it in an exhibition, that will create something new, and we will look at the stone as something potentially interesting. That is what 'Mono' is. My practice is to move beyond the objective aspect of things and to place these things in relation to space and in relation to each other. These relations are important because it is out of them that a space can be liberated, that a space can be opened up. When I introduce a stone into an exhibition, some will ask themselves about the material properties of the thing, about its mass for instance, but for me this gesture constitutes a method.

Q. THE WHITE REVIEW — To my mind the idea of a metaphysics is conceptual. The term metaphysical suggests the existence of a realm of ideas detached from concrete life. So, to clarify, when you use the term metaphysics, do you mean that when you place a thing between parentheses this releases a kind of vital energy, that it produces a new vitality for the thing, recovering a kind of *élan vital*, to borrow an expression from Henri Bergson? Is that what you mean by a metaphysics?

A. LEE UFAN — We cannot really know if there is a vital energy in things, whether by placing them in parentheses or, to take a previous example, by moving a stone into a different context. What is interesting for me is the relation between different things; for instance, to place a steel plate and a stone next to each other and to see what kinds of relations are woven between them as well as the vibrations that they might produce. So when I speak of a metaphysics it is not a metaphysics of the object but a metaphysics of the relations between things. A bottle, for instance, can be placed at an angle or turned upside down to get a slightly different view of it [he lifts a glass bottle from the table and turns it in his hands], and many artists have done this. Yet it is not in the bottle itself that one will encounter a vital force or *élan vital*, but in its rapport with other objects. It is important to say that this experience is not one that is first developed in reflective thought or in words, but is one that finds its beginnings in corporeal experience. These are things that one feels with one's body, which then triggers imaginations.

I spoke earlier of the relationship between stones and steel plates. The issue is of course not as simple as placing these things together. A whole labour of adjustment is required, the labour of bringing these things together, of distancing them, of placing them near a wall, of placing them in proximity to another element. All these small adjustments are the labour that I do as an artist.

Q. THE WHITE REVIEW — Your artistic practice is closely related to your philosophical practice, and throughout your career you have been an eloquent proponent of certain forms of art making. I understand that in the 1960s you were interested in the writings of Martin Heidegger, Maurice Merleau-Ponty and especially Michel Foucault. I don't think that the works you make are reflections of their thoughts, but I'm interested in how these thinkers have contributed to your artistic development.

A. LEE UFAN — I started my studies in Philosophy. That was important to the construction of my identity. But I was born in Asia, so I was also influenced by Eastern thought. And I have travelled a lot, which has also been very important. My work does not stage the thoughts of the philosophers whom you mention. What I did was take from them what interested me, what worked for me. These writers provided references that helped me on my way, but I have never realised their thoughts in my work. My work comprises a dialogue with space, with people, with the environment, with nature. At the beginning of the work there is me, and I try to enter into a relation with the outside world by limiting my ego as much as possible and by listening to what is outside, by listening to what is other. What is important is always to be open to new encounters and to make something out of them.

Q. THE WHITE REVIEW — I certainly didn't mean to say that your works illustrated the ideas of these philosophers. Perhaps I can make my question more precise. In the late

IX

1960s and early 1970s these philosophers – Heidegger was of course from a different period – came to prominence not only because their thinking was new but also because it was political. So I suppose that my question is related to the political stakes of your art making.

A. LEE UFAN —— That is a very good question [laughs]. When we talk about art and its relation to politics we often talk about works that have placed the emphasis on historical events or art that is like propaganda, as in Socialist Realism in Soviet Russia. But the political aspect of art does not stop there, and can be much more profound. When Marcel Duchamp bought a urinal, signed it and turned it into art, the gesture had a very powerful political impact. It broke down received ideas about what art is and what art can be, it made things move. For me, when I do a similar thing by choosing stones and exhibiting them, it is really a way of breaking down received ideas, of renewing the gaze and our relation to art. So I may seem very pure from an artistic point of view, but I think my practice is deeply political in its approach.

Q. THE WHITE REVIEW —— I wonder if we might now turn to the works displayed here at Château la Coste. First HOUSE OF AIR, a work which was installed in 2013, and then your more recent works. I noticed when walking up the path that leads to HOUSE OF AIR that a blurring takes place between the work and the world, that it is difficult to know when the world ends and where the work begins, and vice versa. It is like walking along the length of a Moebius strip. Because there are several stones dotted along the path that are in every respect identical to the stones found elsewhere on the vineyard, except perhaps that these seemed slightly more deliberately placed. It was hard to know if they formed part of the work. Could you talk about this porous relation between the work and the world?

A. LEE UFAN —— I used stones that I found nearby. They are not brought in from the outside or from a different environment but are the kinds of stones that you might find when walking around in the mountains around here. You would have noticed that behind one of these stones I painted a grey shadow on the gravel, and that this stone resembled the others. What I wanted to do here was to make the spectator think about the strangeness of the encounter and to make him or her doubt his or her perception and analysis. This is what I am interested in doing, provoking this kind of reaction in the spectator, a reaction that will undo the distinction between the imaginary and the real, the interior and the exterior. And it is the same with my painted works. In each painting there are spaces that are completely bare, while other parts are painted with a brush. This I hope will make the spectator interrogate the artworks and also create a sense of surprise.

Q. THE WHITE REVIEW —— There is an echo between the central work in your new exhibition, a large stone surrounded by four slightly bent steel tubes, and the position of the spectator in HOUSE OF AIR. The building in this last work is not exactly square. Its sides bulge outwards, creating a sense of expansion, like the diaphragm when you take a deep breath. And I felt something similar when walking around this central work. It is as if the stone were exerting a centrifugal force, as if the steel bars were being pushed outwards.

A. LEE UFAN —— Yes, my practice has to do with feeling how things enter into relations with each other. So instead of placing things in a central position, I prefer to place things in slightly irregular positions so that they can produce different vibrations.

Q. THE WHITE REVIEW —— I understand that this is the first time that you have used colour in your paintings. I noticed when looking at the works exhibited that the red paintings are made with a series of vertical brushstrokes, the blue paintings with a series of horizontal brushstrokes, each producing a different sense of movement. I wondered whether your turn to colour had to do with the particular environment here in Provence, the sky and the sea. I was also thinking of Paul Cézanne's paintings.

A. LEE UFAN —— I cannot say if I have been influenced by this place. I like Cézanne very much and always have him in mind. And it is true that we are in a beautiful region, sunny, clear and colourful. So perhaps, in an unconscious way, I have been influenced by these aspects that you mention and the south of France. Normally I only use a small amount of colour in my work, but this time I made all the paintings using only colour. Perhaps when viewing the works people will think of the relations you mention, and that would be interesting, or they will see things in other ways. For me, though, what is just as important as the painted colours are the parts of the canvases that have not been painted. It is also important to think about how these works create a link or enter into a dialogue with their environment. That is the basis of my practice.

Q. THE WHITE REVIEW —— I am interested in how you have used colour on a technical level. When making paintings without variations of colour, in your monochrome paintings, your use of pigment–based paint allows for the production of differently textured surfaces. Did your use of more oil in these recent coloured paintings produce certain difficulties or problems?

A. LEE UFAN —— With my monochromes I normally use natural pigment made from ground stone. It is a traditional way of painting, and it remains one of the most important parts of my artistic practice. But I recently became interested in the use of colour and so I threw myself into its challenges. The traces left by the brush are not at all the same when you work in monochrome or in colour. In the latter case there is far greater complexity to the mixture of colours and to the traces of the brush. That is why during my recent work with colour there have been several failed works, many more than when I produce monochrome paintings. The difficulties created by colour are very interesting, and this exhibition provided me with a good opportunity to explore them.

There is something else that is important to say about colour, and that is that colour often carries a particular sense or signification. Red carries a certain meaning, blue another, green another still. I do not want the colours to attract all the spectator's attention in these works, so I've tried to achieve a certain neutrality.

Q. THE WHITE REVIEW —— You referred earlier to Marcel Duchamp. It seems to me that, as you say, the most important part of your work is in the relations produced between things and the experiences they invoke. But there is an issue around the process of selection that takes place here. When Duchamp selected his urinal, he did many things, but he also demonstrated how the object entered into another relation, and that relation is economic. A urinal could become an artwork, but the point was also that, given the right circumstances, a urinal could carry an exchange–value that had nothing to do with its qualities as an object. I think your works do something quite different, but I'm interested in your views on the subject. Not so much on the role of the art market in a broad sense, but on the way in which the things you make are things with an economic status.

A· LEE UFAN —— When I spoke of Duchamp earlier I did not mean to say that I admired the artist. It was simply a way of illustrating my point. Personally I am not a fan of his approach because he changes the status of things. He takes a urinal and turns it into an artwork, even though everyone knows that it is just a urinal. This is not an attitude that interests me. In the past, the artist always made the work with his own hands. In an era of industrialisation and automatisation, Duchamp was perhaps the first to show that we have entered a different era and that art can also be the product of industry. But this approach is different to mine because the act of selecting stones or steel plates is my life. I live entirely through this task and this process. Duchamp could have asked a friend to buy a urinal and sign it and the result would have been the same. In my practice, however, there is only me who can make the works I make, because my approach is personal. Then you have the commercial aspect of the work. Of course I sometimes make objects that are sold, though not everything, sometimes things are not sold. But this aspect does not really interest me. What interests me is the process of creating the works. It is my way of living, and it is to this that I am attached.

Q· THE WHITE REVIEW —— A more personal question to end with: what novels are you reading at the moment?

A· LEE UFAN —— I don't read very many contemporary novels. I tried to read Umberto Eco's THE NAME OF THE ROSE, but I stopped halfway because it felt too constructed. It didn't really hold my attention. So I read and re-read the classics: authors like Samuel Beckett, Fyodor Dostoevsky, Marcel Proust, and however many times I re-read them I always have the impression of discovering something new.

RYE DAG HOLMBOE, JULY 2016

THE PIOUS AND
THE POMMERY

BY

ROSANNA MCLAUGHLIN

I.

WHERE IS THE CHAMPAGNE? On second thoughts this is not entirely the right question. The champagne is in the ice trough, on top of the elegantly-worn Eames table behind the partition wall. The woman with a pom–pom on her head milling around beneath the late Frank Stellas has a glass of the stuff, as do the men in overcooked salmon slacks, the eternal *palette du jour* for collectors' trousers, but it doesn't seem likely that any of it is going to make it out of the booth they're standing in, at least not into my hand. Given the circumstances, *Who do I have to be to get a glass of champagne?* might well be the better question.

'Of course if it was up to us, and a lot of people we work with, you know, it would just be open to everyone the whole time,' Matthew Slotover, co-founder of Frieze Art Fair, had told me some weeks prior, a little unconvincingly. Because at 7 p.m. on 14 October, 2015, standing in the aisle of London's most lucrative contemporary art fair on the opening night, the meticulously planned tiering system is as clear as the shoreline under the Saint-Tropez sun. Slotover has given me a 5 p.m. VIP pass, which in the Frieze running order makes me a fourth-class citizen. Above me are the VVIPs, who can access the tent from 2 p.m.; above them are the VVVIPs, free to mill around from midday; and above them are the VVVVIPs, persons of paramount importance who can enter the tent from 11 a.m., and are furnished upon arrival with a complimentary bag of beauty products. The 5 p.m. VIP pass, then, is for persons of distinctly ordinary importance.

But not to despair, because although I am only fourth on the ladder there are many more beneath me. There are the eager groups of art students sneaking in on the ticket of an art world friend, only to realise, once zapped through the guarded bag check, that Princess Eugenie is back in her castle, Benedict Cumberbatch has left the tent, and the champagne, that damn champagne, is anything but forthcoming. And then there are the 80 per cent of visitors to the fair who actually *pay* to get in, visitors who are also subjected to the rigours of tiering. *Be the first to see Frieze!* the website rather disingenuously advertises the Premium ticket, available at an extra cost on Wednesday when the fair first opens to the great and uninvited. By Saturday the collectors have cleared out their luggage from the cloakroom and departed the tent entirely, en route to Dubai or Moscow, having enjoyed the benefits of their 'non-domiciled' status, a boon to the city's high-rolling international residents that makes splashing out at the fair particularly appealing. Or off to Paris's Grand Palais for the opening of FIAC, the next fair in the calendar, where many of the galleries at Frieze London will once again lay out their wares, before moving on to Cologne, Miami, New York, Hong Kong... or back across the park to the mansion houses of Primrose Hill for that matter, making way for the hoi polloi of London's culture-curious on Regent's Park's lawns.

If on Tuesday the fair is a chin-tuck in Dior brogues, by the weekend it's a schoolgirl with a Winsor & Newton sketchbook, diligently cross-hatching her way through a sculpture in the booth opposite, without noticing that seen from behind it is not, in fact, the sincere mid-century meditation on the union of landscape and female form she thinks it is, but a gigantic bronze penis, penetrating itself through its own, Henry Moore-esque orifice; if only she had taken the time to walk around the thing, but she was put off by that rather stiff-looking Parisian gallerist in a tailored suit and trainer shoes, the one doing his utmost to appear as if he were alone with his MacBook in the 6th Arrondissement, waiting for a collector to arrive for a *vue intime*. Perspective, alas, is not something one learns from still-life lessons alone...

Art fairs have a habit of showing everyone present in an unsympathetic light. Because, of course, the gallerist is not there to offer free tours to school children but to sell art, and has stumped up a five-figure sum for a booth in a prime location, money that will not be repaid by acts of benevolent pedagogy. And that girl studying the bronze, has she not in fact arrived with the rather commendable notion that one might *learn* something from art, and was she not also enticed to the tent by Frieze itself, which publicises the fair as a place to buy art, yes, but also as a glittering pin thumbed into the map of the cultural landscape? 'Experience moments of immersion and interaction,' says the press material, 'encounter impressive outdoor works,' 'explore Frieze Projects, the fair's non-profit programme of artists' commissions.' *Experience, encounter, discover, explore*, words tailored to an altogether different audience than *buy, sell, network* and *speculate*.

Herein lies the crux of Frieze London. It is everything all at once, trade fair and cultural institution, commercial and non-profit, a fair that commissions artists at the same time that it is paid by galleries to show them. Frieze is a microcosm of the art world from the fringes to the moneyed core, and reveals all its dazzling paradoxes.

These were paradoxes, I decided, that I should like to get to the bottom of. And so, in the run-up to the 2015 edition of Frieze London, I spoke to three people who have been involved in the fair from its inception – the former Young British Artist Jake Chapman, super-collector Candida Gertler, and the co-founder of Frieze Art Fair, Matthew Slotover – as well as a number of newcomers and casualties, in order to track the various beliefs and investments that follow artworks as they pass through the heart of the market.

II.

'When I go to Frieze I think a lot about the idea that if there was an overnight virus and everyone died, and the Martians came down and started trying to catalogue what the fuck people were up to, you know, there would be certain things they could say *yep, yep, absolutely, we get that*.' Jake Chapman breaks off from his story, one of many he would tell me over the course of an afternoon at his gated studio complex in Hackney Wick, and picks up the glass in front of him as an example. 'But there'd be certain things they'd be looking at saying *what the fuck is this?*' I ask whether the aliens would approve of the artworks he makes with his older brother and collaborator, Dinos. 'It wouldn't last. Ours wouldn't, no!' Would the aliens not understand, I enquire, the artworks they produced? 'I think they would understand them, they'd think children made them! Weird children, very disturbed children.'

Jake Chapman is a big man. His face is peppered with stubble, where his head is not bald it is shaved close to the skull, and his arms are covered in scrappy homemade tattoos. When we meet he is dressed in a camouflage t-shirt, jeans and heavy leather boots. But despite his imposing figure, there is something disarmingly innocent about him. His eyebrows point upwards in the middle in an expression of mild and pleasant surprise, he is prone to debilitating bouts of giggles, and while his rampant verbosity might be unbearable in someone else, even the most convoluted of tales are turned sweet on Chapman's lips, tales which he delivers with the freedom and gaiety of a bird singing in a tree. These qualities combine in him, so that whatever the argument he is busy extolling, whether Armageddon or the existential crisis of the artwork at an art fair, he gives the impression that his spirit, for all the world, is as light as cotton candy. Here is a man able to be at once deadly serious and completely infantile, and who has built a career out of this particular capacity.

'I remember Matthew Slotover and Tom Gidley coming up to me years and years and years ago, and they gave me a little piece of paper, a little photocopy,' Chapman tells me, breaking into a very silly voice. 'And they came up and they said, *we're gonna do a...* they were really little, you know... *we're gonna do this magazine, it's gonna be called* frieze, *and we're wondering if you'd like to write for it.* And I remember thinking, ah, that's sweet. And look at it now.'

The Frieze empire began with *FRIEZE* magazine – founded by Slotover, Amanda Sharp and artist Tom Gidley in 1991 – and rose to prominence with the Young British Artists – a group whose swaggering, shock-baiting antics featured heavily in the early editions, and who now command vast sums on the international market. The Chapman brothers are among those associated with the YBA moniker who went on to become household names, along with the galleries and dealers who made them. Jay Jopling, owner of White Cube gallery, continues to represent the Chapmans to their mutual benefit; he also launched the careers of Damien Hirst and Tracey Emin. Jopling was never a poor man – the son of a Conservative Baron, he was educated at Eton – but his estimated fortune of £100 million has certainly been bolstered by White Cube's commercial success. 'I always liked to collide the establishment with the avant-garde,' he said of his *modus operandi* in an interview with the *FINANCIAL TIMES*' art critic Jackie Wullschlager. 'In art world terms,' Wullschlager explains,

Jopling '*is* the establishment.'

Chapman tells me that he wrote for FRIEZE magazine on a number of occasions, but stopped after deciding that the magazine was too 'humane' and 'confessional'. One of Damien Hirst's now trademark butterfly pictures featured on the cover of the first edition – a staple-bound magazine with a flimsy, callow charm. By the time that the 174th edition came out in October 2015, the magazine had a print readership of 320,000, and three of the world's most prominent art fairs had opened under the Frieze umbrella: Frieze London, Frieze Masters, which joins the original fair on the lawns of Regent's Park, and Frieze New York.

Shortly before the opening of Frieze London 2015, I visit Matthew Slotover at Frieze HQ, on the top floor of a converted Victorian poor school in Shoreditch. The door to his glass-walled office opens, and Slotover rises with a slow, broad smile. He looks good, a trim figure with dark, close-cropped hair who shows little evidence of approaching 50. To the right of his desk is a lounge area of mid-century furniture in black leather and dark hardwood. A rubberised pannier bag unclipped from Slotover's bicycle is propped against the wall, and strapped to his wrist, catching the light as it cascades through the Victorian window panes, is the blank, glossy face of the latest Apple smart watch.

The initial idea for FRIEZE, he says, was to 'promote young artists and sell their work directly through the magazine', but the plan changed when he was advised that wasn't how the industry worked, 'that you go through the galleries and there's a reason for that', and that it would be 'tacky' to sell art through a publication. A nascent contemporary art magazine, of course, would considerably hamper its chances of success by cutting out galleries, the same art world professionals who form an integral part of FRIEZE's readership, and who shell out upwards of £3,000 for a full page advertisement (advertisements which, in 2015's November edition, account for roughly half of the magazine's content). The initial idea to sell art through the magazine was not so much dropped as re-calibrated. Page space and not artworks would be the object in which FRIEZE traded, allowing artists and galleries to become 'friends', as Slotover calls them, rather than direct competitors. 'Doing a magazine', he tells me, 'you get to know artists, you become sympathetic towards them. Of course you're supposed to be critical about them but generally you're on their side. And if something's not interesting, we just don't cover it.'

It would not be until 2003 that Frieze London first pitched its gargantuan white tent on Regent's Park's lawns, but the seeds for the magazine's expansion had been sown some years prior. In 1995, FRIEZE published an article by photographer Collier Schorr titled 'Who is the Fairest of Them All'. 'The art fair', Schorr opens, 'is the most frequented and beleaguered event manufactured by the art world.' Full of moustachioed dealers wearing braces and monk shoes, she suggested they were

E

no place for the future faces of the market. There was, however, an exception – for Schorr, and significantly for the young Matthew Slotover – and it came in the form of UnFair.

UnFair was established in 1992 by a group of galleries who had been denied booths by a dinosaur of the fair circuit, the prestigious and long-running Art Cologne. Unlike Art Cologne, held in the great trade fair halls on the edge of the city, UnFair took place in a disused department store in the centre of town. The stuffy old world had been banished; this fair had renegade status.

Slotover recalls UnFair fondly. 'They had Motown playing over the tannoy,' he tells me, 'and Damien Hirst was at the tiny White Cube stand, and he put twins sitting on the stand next to twin frankfurters in formaldehyde – *because it was in Cologne*,' he says, grinning. It was at UnFair that the YBAs began to shine in the eyes of the international market; it was at UnFair that the market place could, at long last, be cool.

Gregor Muir, now the director of London's ICA gallery, remembers UnFair through similarly rebel-tinted spectacles. 'I hitched a ride to Cologne with FRIEZE magazine,' he writes in his memoir LUCKY KUNST: THE RISE AND FALL OF YOUNG BRITISH ART, with none other than a young Slotover behind the wheel. After an encounter with an artist pretending to be unpacked from a shipping crate, who 'delivered a thigh-slapping proclamation that he would continue to live in his crate for the duration of the fair', Muir headed to the opening party with Jake Chapman.

'The atmosphere was exhilarating,' Muir continues, 'everyone dancing to the thumping beats that reverberated through the vast interior. I looked up from my triple vodka and tonic and saw Anthony Reynolds, an otherwise reserved London gallerist, boogying on the dance floor'. The night did not end there. At two in the morning, Muir and Chapman returned to the fair, arriving the picture of rebellion, 'utterly inebriated' and covered in crumbs 'from the collection of cakes we'd stuffed in our mouths after passing a bakery preparing for the day ahead'. Once inside, Muir helped himself to beer from behind the bar, and Chapman began swapping the paintings between booths – that is until Muir intervened, fearing their antics would provoke such grave retribution that the pair would be 'deported'.

UnFair ended after only two years, but it showed that at a fair one really could have it all – boogying gallerists, pickled wieners, performance artists, and no end of minor rebellions. Best of all, like an anarchist fancy-dress party in a hedge-fund office, was the potential to have all this while making vast sums of money.

'We would go to the art fairs in Cologne', Slotover tells me, 'and Basel and Paris and Madrid, and think, "Wow, these are great". And we would go there as art critics to try and find out about the art, and meet the dealers, and see what artists were doing. So we always thought art fairs were great places, not thinking at all about the buying and selling of it, just as a way of communicating.' The first Frieze fair was unveiled in

2003, with 124 galleries from across the world participating. By the end of the week, £20 million of sales had taken place within the tent, with Frieze making just shy of £1 million from renting out floor space alone.

III.

The Chapman brothers have been frequent exhibitors at Frieze Art Fair since its inception, showing in the blue-chip section at the front of the tent. If access to the fair is subject to a strict tiering process, so too is the tent's topography, with galleries organised alphabetically into zones from front to back according to status. Up the ramp at the entrance, drop off your luggage, through security, locate your zone... Universal Studio, the firm who designed the tent, are masters in the art of transforming corporate non-space into a luxury destination. Also on their résumé: the Fortnum & Mason Champagne Bar at Heathrow's Terminal 5.

The bulk of exhibitors – commercially established galleries working with commercially established artists – are in the Main Stand, with the blue-chippers in the A zone by the entrance where the cost of floor space enters five figures. Such outlays can be recuperated in a single sale: at White Cube's stand in 2015, Damien Hirst's painting *HOLBEIN (ARTIST'S WATERCOLOURS)* (2015) sold for just shy of a million before lunchtime on the opening day.

At the back of the tent, bringing up the rear in zones G and H, is the Focus section for younger galleries. Here careers are less established, business more precarious, floor space is cheaper and there is pressure, particularly on debutante galleries, to show artworks of a less straightforwardly commercial nature. 'If you want to get in the club', artist Samara Scott tells me, having embedded a pond of fizzy drinks, shampoo and various perishable matter directly into the floor of the tent for the maiden voyage at Frieze of the gallery that represents her, South London's Sunday Painter, 'you have to do a difficult initiation act.' Once the hazing is over, a gallery can pull out the plinths, hang the paintings, and take the easier route to making sales. But 'it would be distasteful', Scott says, 'for a young, upcoming gallery to do something so – *oh my god! transparently commercial, how disgusting!*'

One of the Chapmans' most memorable outings at Frieze London was *PAINTING FOR PLEASURE AND PROFIT* in 2006, for which they set up shop in White Cube's booth painting half an hour portraits for £4,500 a pop. 'I could see what Dinos was doing,' Chapman says of this venture, 'he could see what I was doing, but the people sitting couldn't see, so we'd do two people at the same time, and it was the funniest. He did the most beautiful, really beautiful, *exquisite* painting of this demure Spanish woman who sat down, paid her money – and it was not an insubstantial amount – and he painted her and she had this lovely necklace and beautiful silk dress, and he painted this. And then he painted this severed neck!' Chapman's face concertinas in giggles;

E

evidently, he is immensely pleased by the memory of the decapitated subject. 'Just the idea of sitting down and *not* getting your portrait done!'

The demure Spanish woman in the silk dress would have been disappointed, of course, if the Chapmans hadn't come up with something suitably puckish. The pair thrive on playing the court jester, of presenting the apparently unpresentable to their audience. Among their biggest feats to date are buying a set of Francisco Goya's DISASTERS OF WAR etchings from the early nineteenth century and defacing them for an exhibition at White Cube in 1999, and adding rainbows and love hearts to watercolours painted by Adolf Hitler – at least ostensibly, the pair have form when it comes to the art world hoax – for their exhibition IF HITLER HAD BEEN A HIPPY HOW HAPPY WE WOULD BE at White Cube in 2008. Gruesome portraits to order, by their standards, are relatively tame fare. At 2007's fair they were back at White Cube offering to deface £20 and £50 notes for fairgoers, free of charge – an exhibit that Candida Gertler, art collector and founder of philanthropic organisation OUTSET, described as among her favourite exhibits to date.

I met Gertler at the Greenberry Cafe in Primrose Hill to find out more about the tightly entwined genesis of OUTSET and Frieze London, as well as the curious attraction of the super-rich to the 'non-profit' sides of the art world. With her ringed fingers sparkling in the North-West London sun, Gertler eased into an origin story of how she, Sharp and Slotover had concocted the plan while out for dinner one night 'in a little Korean restaurant' in 2002. The details of this story were evidently important, as if the smallness of the restaurant and the fact that it was Korean displayed not only the intimate relationship she had with Sharp and Slotover, but a subtler form of sophistication. When one could very well eat every meal at the Ritz, it is those things which not only have to be paid for but discovered that are the mark of the truly cultivated.

They hatched a plan: to create a fund of money – £150,000, made up of individual pledges from private donors in Gertler's network of friends and associates – with which artworks would be bought at Frieze London and donated directly to the national collection at Tate. One of the artworks on OUTSET's shopping list for 2004's fair, Roman Ondák's GOOD FEELINGS IN GOOD TIMES (2003), would become the first work of performance art ever owned by the Tate. Ondak's piece consisted of performers instructed to line up in queues between seven and fourteen strong, reading papers, twiddling their thumbs, in areas of the fair where one might not expect a queue to form.

GOOD FEELINGS IN GOOD TIMES was exhibited as a part of the non-profit Frieze Projects, a section of the fair Gertler describes as showing '*less obviously commercially viable*' artworks. Unlike the majority of artists participating in the fair, whose work is displayed in booths paid for by the galleries that represent them, artists showing as part of Frieze Projects are commissioned by in–house curators to produce site–specific work. Dotted around the tent as a series of theatrical and participatory interludes, the Projects bring to the fair something missing from the rows of paintings and objects on plinths which – typically having little to no conceptual relationship with the tent, the artworks they are displayed alongside or the fair itself – appear ready to be packed up and shipped on. The Projects take seriously the fair's ambition to be a space of curatorial as well as financial value; they make Frieze appear less like a bazaar and more like an exhibition.

'There was no price tag to it,' Gertler tells me, recounting the purchase of Ondak's work, 'and I remember standing in the corridor with Jessica Morgan' – then the Curator of Contemporary Art at Tate Modern – 'who was at the time part of our team, and Roman said "I don't have a price for it," and then they disappeared, and you know, there was two minutes of conversation, and they came back with "£8,000". OK! £8,000!'

Gertler's excitement at having bought an artwork without a price tag was palpable. But in reality, buying a performance work from the non–profit section of the fair is like asking a shopkeeper if you can buy the jacket on the mannequin in the window. It might not be the obvious choice, it might be, as Gertler so aptly put it, less obviously commercially viable, but it is a request that is hardly likely to be denied. A shop is a shop, a market is a market, a fair is a fair, and for the right price everything is for sale.

There is evidently an appeal in aligning oneself with artworks that have a less explicit relationship with commerce. Like that *little Korean restaurant*, such artworks offer something that the big names of the art market do not. When having the bank balance of a multi–millionaire is qualification enough to hang a *Spot Painting* by Damien Hirst in the stateroom of your superyacht, buying the ostensibly un–buyable is an especially piquant pleasure. By this logic, it is perhaps unsurprising that when Gertler lists her favourite exhibits at Frieze to date, the list should include three exhibits that are *less obviously commercially viable*, and which all also involved waiting in line – an experience of thrilling mundanity, one can only assume, for those unacquainted with Lidl on a Sunday afternoon. In addition to Ondák's queue and the Chapman's defaced bank notes, topping Gertler's list is rolling down a grass slope as part of Paola Pivi's installation for the Projects section in 2003, a popular attraction that required a brief spell of the much enjoyed hanging around.

IV.

The Chapman brothers have been granted the keys to Frieze City, and in his studio, Jake Chapman runs me through a number of convoluted and improbable suggestions they have floated concerning their participation. 'We wanted to do a booth where you could go and buy someone else's work from somewhere else and bring it to us and

E

we'd change it.' The flaw in this proposal, alas, was 'the unpredictability of people's egos'. Another idea involved offering 'free money' to homeless people at the fair. For this, he tells me, 'we'd need to have an ATM, we'd have us drawing, and what people would have to do is take out £20, give homeless people £10 and we'd draw.' But the mother of all proposals, also including the unsuspecting homeless, was one suggested to Miuccia Prada, head of the luxury goods dynasty, a major patron of the arts.

'We had another idea to do a show in Milan at the Prada Foundation, and I just remember sitting and talking to Miuccia Prada and suggesting this as a possible idea. It was called TRAMPS ON ICE. We wanted to build a big ice rink – because Milan is full of smackheads and a terrible sort of drug population, sub-population – and we'd say if you come there you'd get some money and a free dinner. But you have to ice skate for an hour. I mean it's hugely fascistic but the idea was that when they arrive, they skate for an hour, and then they have a shower, then when they come out we take their clothes, we put them on a hanger and put Prada labels in their clothes, they get Prada clothes, they get a meal and then they leave. So the show's on for three months, the clothes would get less and less worn because the same people would be coming and bringing back Prada clothes and getting fresh Prada clothes. We'd bottle the shower water and call it *Eau de Tramp*, and the by-product is that these drug addicts would end up being brilliant ice skaters. Win win! Obviously they didn't really go for that.'

There was, however, 'lots of laughing'. And that, of course, is precisely the point. Neither Frieze nor the Prada Foundation – a cultural organisation with a permanent exhibition space in Milan, in a building designed by Rem Koolhaas, one part of which is clad in 24-carat gold leaf – were going to entertain ideas that poke such extensive fun at the conspicuous wealth behind their operations. Not to mention allowing the homeless through their doors, which at Frieze would require extending the fair for at least another week, in order to make space for all the rungs on the social ladder between the VVVVIPs and the destitute – but both were no doubt pleased to be in on the merriment, just as the demure Spanish lady would have been pleased with her severed head. This is the particular appeal of the Chapman brothers. Not only do they have license to mock the cultural aristocracy, but the aristocracy actively enjoy it – it adds a little *frisson* to proceedings.

V.

In large part, the Chapmans' prolonged success is down to having mastered a defining characteristic of the contemporary art industry: the fine art of double-tracking. To double-track is to be both: counter-cultural and establishment, uptown and downtown, an exotic addition to the dinner table who still knows how to find their way around the silverware. The exemplary double-tracker, wrote Tom Wolfe in THE PAINTED WORD in 1975, arrives at a private view at MoMA in a dinner jacket and paint splattered Levis, exclaiming '*I'm still a virgin!* (Where's the champagne?)'

Art is a decidedly social industry, where business doubles-up as pleasure; an industry in which clients are friends. Accordingly, collectors don't just want the clay or the paint or pound shop dreck transformed into cultural gold, they often want a relationship with the alchemist too. And so, as much as artists ply their trade in the studio, they must also ply it on the social circuit, enabling the rich to journey vicariously to the exotic lands of the (relatively speaking) poor, without ever mentioning the arms or the oil or the property portfolios that bankroll such boutique vacations, or the promise of money that explains why the artist is present in the situation at all. 'I feel at times like a weird escort,' Samara Scott told me shortly after the 2015 fair, smarting from the pressure of having to socialise with potential business interests. 'I mean you don't have to sleep with them, but there's an exchange that you have to give.'

Frieze London's own flair for double-tracking reached its zenith at 2015's talks programme, organised by the Lucky Kunst himself, Gregor Muir. The talks covered a range of subjects from the social impact of museums to the imprisonment of art activists and the legacy of punk. But the stand-out event was a panel discussion, titled 'Off-Centre: Can Artists Still Afford to Live in London?'

The event was so popular that tickets had to be reserved in advance, and attendees were advised to arrive twenty minutes early. Behind me as I waited in line a young man in a fur hat and a brocaded coat so long that it tickled his ankles knocked back a mid-afternoon glass of champagne. By this point the entire queue ought to have known, in fact should have known already, why the talk we were yet to see was flawed. For there may be many artists struggling to afford the cost of London living, and many non-artists for that matter who cannot afford the rise in rent ushered in by the influx of artists, who set up studios in poorer areas of the city, shortly to be followed by coffee shops and craft breweries and property developers, but not one of those people was to be found among the fur hats and the £36 entrance tickets. Nevertheless, such a dose of political engagement makes for a bracing digestif, following those Serrano ham croquettes in the VIP lounge.

Double-tracking is not only a pious mask to cover the whims of the wealthy. It is the thing that allows us all to appreciate the painting on the gallery wall without being deluged by the thought of the machinations and the millions that led to it hanging there. It is what enables us to engage with the world not in its unsavoury entirety, but as an artist presents it to us, and as we ourselves would like to see it. Without it, it is questionable whether there could be any art appreciation at all. What distinguishes double-tracking from its less discerning relatives – the flip-floppers and the U-turners and the outright conmen – is that it cannot be easily faked or fudged. For the gallery, for the artist, for the middle-men and for the viewer alike, double-tracking requires dedication, and most importantly of all, it requires *belief*.

E

As a sign of the significance of this faith, it must be upheld even in the most explicitly commercial contexts. It is something that Frieze insists be carried out throughout the fair, right down to the selection process. Following 2015's fair I spoke with Barnie Page, director of the London gallery Limoncello. Page told me he knew a number of figures on the London commercial scene who had applied repeatedly to get into Frieze London, but were routinely rejected. The reason, he told me, was that they were seen as 'dealers' and not 'gallerists'. While a gallerist is both a businessperson and a pious servant of the arts – a gallerist must be able to vouch for the quality, and not just the marketability, of the artworks they promote – to be branded a 'dealer' is to be tarnished by purely avaricious interests. It is to adhere, and fatally, to only a single track.

VI.

In 2010, Matthew Slotover took part in a debate at the Saatchi Gallery. The motion: 'Art Fairs Are About Money Not Art'. Slotover, in the 'no' camp along with artist Richard Wentworth and critic Norman Rosenthal, was pitched against Louisa Buck of THE ART NEWSPAPER, artist and writer Matthew Collings, and a then-painter named Jasper Joffe.

Joffe was present because he had set up The Free Art Fair, a short lived, alternative model of fair at which artworks were not sold but given away at the end via an elaborate raffle. 'For once', reads the now obsolete press material, 'instead of art going to the highest bidder or those who can afford it, someone who really loves an artwork will be able to have it for free.' The Free Art Fair had some limited success: of its three incarnations, one was held at the Barbican Centre, and it attracted a number of well-known artists, including Bob and Roberta Smith and Joffe's sister, the painter Chantal Joffe.

At the debate focus inevitably shifted to Frieze, and Joffe – the least known of the group and evidently the least proficient in the etiquette of debating – lost his cool. Anger tuned his voice, his ample curls were furiously smoothed against his skull, and his cheeks flushed crimson. His main gripes: Frieze exhibits more men than it does women, the selection process is run by a cartel of gallerists, and that by pandering to the tastes of the rich, Frieze does a disservice to the majority of underpaid artists.

Slotover responded coolly, adhering to rule number one of debating: that showing one's emotions is a mistake on par with a fox offering its bottom to the hounds to sniff. He began by pointing out the history of unequal representation at Joffe's own fair, listing the disproportionate number of male participants from The Free Art Fair's press material, before reminding the audience that 80 per cent of visitors to Frieze Art Fair come to spectate and not to buy. Hardly, he argued, a statistic befitting an avaricious cartel.

Later that same year, an artwork of Joffe's was removed from Frieze London. London radio station Resonance FM had been invited to participate in Frieze Projects, and planned to use their booth to hold an auction as a fundraiser. One of the intended lots was a painting by Joffe of a po-faced Nicholas Serota, director of Tate, with the words 'Cheer Up Love' painted in the background amid a sea of polka dots. Frieze removed the painting before the auction began, citing the fair's 'strict policy of selection'. 'I presume', said Joffe at the time to the INDEPENDENT newspaper, doing his best to at least go down in flames, 'it is because I was recently in a debate at the Saatchi Gallery with Matthew Slotover, and he seemed quite upset and angry that I criticised Frieze.'

I mention to Slotover that I had seen this debate. Joffe, he tells me, had made a 'big deal' about their confrontation afterwards. He 'edited my Wikipedia page to make it really big, and stuff like that. It's all been a bit... *stalkery*.' And, as a final nail in poor Joffe's coffin, 'not being selected, I think, was his main problem.' This seems a rather cruel dispatching of the subject, cruel, because it was no doubt true. *If something's not interesting we just don't cover it,* Slotover said of the magazine's selection policy, and at the fair, as it is at the magazine, not being selected is a judgement that offers little room for reply.

'Facts', wrote Aldous Huxley, 'do not cease to exist because they are ignored.' The same cannot be said for careers in the arts. A week prior to meeting Matthew Slotover, I had breakfast with Joffe. At his suggestion we met in a co-operative cafe in Hackney, the day before it was due to shut down. Over rye bread toast and fair-trade coffee Joffe spent an hour expounding on the evils of the art world, revealing that he has subsequently quit art altogether, setting up in publishing instead. The narrative of being a dangerous agitator excluded from the market, a Guevara to Slotover's Kennedy, disarmed of his aggravating spotty canvases, evidently suited him well – just as it suited Slotover to write Joffe off as 'stalkery'.

'I would question people who feel they're excluded from Frieze. Are they excluded from other fairs as well, that have nothing to do with us?' Slotover reasons, considering from the apex of the golden ladder the man who has slipped down a snake to the bottom of the board. 'Unfortunately, a lot of the time you come to the same conclusions. And not through any collusions because it's not in anyone's interest. So, you know, it's competitive. But life is competitive!'

VII.

Slotover's fondness for broadcasting that 80 per cent of Frieze Art Fair's visitors come as spectators and not buyers is a masterstroke of double-tracking, which does much to reframe the fair as something other than a trading floor. It is a statistic that can be found repeated in numerous publications. THE NEW YORK TIMES have it, THE

SPECTATOR too. It is even cited, no less, in the first lines of Frieze Art Fair's Wikipedia page. And come the non-buying spectatorship do, for there is nowhere better to see a comprehensive who's who of the commercial art world. The fair provides an annual survey of the artists and artistic trends at the forefront of the international market. It also provides an opportunity to witness gallerists and collectors in action, those agents of the commercial art world so often invisible to the gallery-going public, and so often just out of reach for aspiring artists.

What was not listed on Frieze's Wikipedia page was the pleasure of arriving at the fair as one of the 20 per cent, with the sole purpose of spending large sums of money. And so at Frieze HQ, I ask Slotover perhaps the most obvious question of all. Why is buying an artwork better than simply looking at it? 'Well, like you I never used to own it, partly because I couldn't afford it – but you know there are editions and things that one can buy that are not expensive,' he says, graciously empathising with my financial status, before taking the opportunity to advertise the cheaper end of the market. 'When you go to a fair it takes on a different atmosphere when it's like, "OK, I'm gonna buy something." There's an excitement about it, and you're looking at art with that view, so it's like, "OK, what do we like, how much is it, is it available?" And you kind of have a motive, you know, a mission. And then you buy it and the dealer's really happy and the artist's really happy, and then you get it shipped home or you take it home, and you find somewhere in your house for it, and you look at it every day. And then a year later you might move it around, brighten up a room that was a bit dull or boring before, and it's amazing.'

The dealer's happy, the artist's happy, the new owner's happy – the art fair, according to this description, is at least a peaceable kingdom.

The suckling child may well be playing on the hole of the asp, or have his hand in the cockatrice's den for that matter, but only, one suspects, because he has learnt to tolerate the poison. Slotover's vision of the fair is a far cry from that of British artist Jesse Wine, who first showed at Frieze Art Fair in 2013 with his London gallery Limoncello, and who entered the proceedings by way of a baptism of fire. In order to secure their place in the Focus section of the tent, dedicated to younger galleries, Limoncello proposed that the three young men they were exhibiting would be present in the booth alongside their work for the entire duration of the week.

It is highly unusual for an artist to man their own booth. After overseeing the installation of their work, if indeed their oversight is required, artists appear tentatively in the tent – at the private view, to meet with collectors or journalists at the request of their gallery, or to take a furtive, midweek glance at what else is on display. (A case in point. When I ask Jake Chapman if he will be participating in 2015's fair, he replies with the sort of nonchalance that is the sole preserve of the firmly established: 'I think Jay will probably drag something down there.') Unless an artist is

E

in a position of power so considerable that they are able to demand complete control over the manner in which their work enters into circulation, they keep their presence to a minimum and for good reason. 'Artists don't make art to make sales,' Wine tells me, but at Frieze, the boundary that distinguishes an artwork from a commodity, and for that matter an artist from an escort, is in serious danger of dissolving.

This, then, was a masterstroke for a young gallery: to say to the beast how beautiful it is, what a pleasure its company. Abercrombie & Fitch may employ the services of shirtless, six-packing gym bunnies to entice customers into their stores, but they've got nothing on the appeal of three fresh-faced colts at an art fair, instructed to be as available as possible and no doubt rendered desperate by the task at hand. For six days Wine stood in the booth, enticing the passing crowds to stop for a while, to take a seat with him on one of the chairs provided with such *tête-à-têtes* in mind. 'I just sort of thought,' he says of the experience, 'if I look the devil in the eye a little bit with this art fair stuff, and am present and see exactly how it works, and see the emotional transaction and the financial transaction take place, then I won't be able to be disturbed by it.'

VIII.

Speak to any artist who has exhibited at an art fair, and they will likely tell you that while the conditions for display are far from ideal, participating is necessary if you intend to make a living. Speak to any gallerist, and they will likely tell you their business depends upon it. 'The one thing that I would say that really makes sense,' Wine says of mounting a commercially successful booth at Frieze, 'is to be consistent in your display. Because it's the same as when you go to a shoe shop. You don't see a pair of stilettos next to a pair of Timberlands next to a pair of flip-flops. You don't see that. You see four different colours of Timberlands. Because then you've got a choice, but within a confined environment. And I think that's how the fair operates, that's why the people with the display which turns over the most cash – and that is obviously the goal of it – are the ones that fucking treat it as a normal commercial environment.'

London gallery Stuart Shave Modern Art is no stranger to the logic of the shoe shop. In 2015 it was declared winner of the Pommery Champagne Stand Prize, receiving as its reward £10,000 and a bottle of Pommery the size of a small child. On the walls of its booth were five works by artist Mark Flood, identically sized and evenly spaced in a range of colours, each a pixellated image of a Mark Rothko painting. Here, surely, is that *choice within a confined environment*, a reproduction of a popular product for sale in bubblegum pinks and greens, as well as deep purple and midnight blue for the more soberly inclined. And on the floor of the booth, a line of sculptures by Yngve Holen – seven washing machines, each topped with a warped sheet of plexiglass, and model aeroplanes pointing in various directions. The masterful control of minor differences – the choice between an aeroplane pointing East or West, of plexiglass bent upwards or plexiglass bent down – and of course the domestic scale they offered to Flood's Rothko's – useful as an indication of how they might fit in back home – ensured the stand was triumphant. No mention of the 'different-colours-of-Timberland-boots' approach was made by the judging panel, who praised instead the 'intellectual and formal dialogue', but one can only assume it had been tacitly acknowledged.

With the financial stakes so high for artists and galleries alike, and with certain types of artwork proving bankable, it does not take a huge leap of the imagination to see how the art fair has begun to dictate the nature of artworks being produced. This idea was given short shrift at Frieze HQ. 'Look,' Slotover tells me, 'I think it's your duty as an artist to make the best work you possibly can. And to follow your interests and your dreams and whatever.' But, 'if the gallery is exerting pressure on you as an artist to make work that you don't think is good, well, there's no gun to your head. It's your decision. If a gallery says, "Oh, I quite like that piece but can you make it smaller, and in pink, because we could sell it?" you've got a choice. Either you say "Great, I'd love some money this month, and if you think so, I'll do one in pink." Or you can say "How dare you tell me what to make. I'm off, I'm going with another who's not going to do that." Eventually, it's down to the artist. And all artists have to think about it. "Am I interested in selling stuff, do I want the market to follow me or me to follow it?"'

I ask Jake Chapman about the experience of exhibiting at an art fair, and he replies with characteristic merriment. 'When you go to Frieze and you see the scale of things, and you see the works in such a homogenised environment – in a sense you get to see how hopeless a work of art is, as a thing which can actually fulfil all of the things you want it to do when you're in the process of making the thing. And that's easier to have when objects can gang up on the viewer, when there are enough objects or enough paintings that can build some kind of cosmology of meaning based on their context. But when it's one thing, then another thing, then another thing, it's like watching the existential crisis of the work of art, not being able to actually get away with what it's supposed to do.'

Shorn of any affinity with their surroundings bar commerce, Chapman concludes, all artworks can be at the fair are 'little punctuation marks in someone's journey through this screaming forest of little existential objects which are just so totally orphaned, because their meaning is attached to context'. I recount this rather bleak appraisal to Matthew Slotover, who replies with an act of double-tracking *par excellence*. 'That's very good', he says. 'Did he write that or did he come out with that?' When I tell him it came straight out of Chapman's mouth, he is evidently extremely pleased. 'Really? That's excellent!'

E

DO YOU WANT TO DIP THE RAT

BY

DOROTHEA LASKY

DO YOU WANT TO DIP THE RAT

Do you want to dip the rat
Completely in oil

Do you want to dip the rat
Before we eat it eat it

Do you want to dip the rat
Completely in oil

Before we eat it

Tender tender meat
Like pork shoulder

A hundred traps set
Eighty hanging in a row to be broiled

With you
I'd take it raw

Tiny pink feet
Glistening with oil

Legs and feet
Glistening with oil

Matted fur and face
Weighted down with oil

Everything in oil
But the teeth are shiny clean

No what I really want to know
Before you open that mouth again

Should we completely dip the rat in oil

Before we eat it eat it

Should we completely
Dip the rat in oil

Before we eat it

TWIN PEAKS

I'm sadly just pure instinct in a jeans jacket
A guess in a red dress
I only have time for coffee
But do you
Have time
For me

Shadow cousin
With the face
Of my past abuser
Cough cough and a little
Whatever

My pussy squirts flowers
In the spring
Purple hair
And all that jazz
Like a tear

The moon is in Scorpio
I'm
In
The moon
My
Baby
Moon
My baby

I am still
Despite it all
Milking
Do you want me
Do you want to
Sip my clear
Cocoon
Full of nutrients

Sadly still only a
Summative
Mountaintop
Do you want to soak it
Completely in oil
Before we eat it
Glistening
The tiny pink feet

Do you want to soak
The rat
Completely
In oil
Before
We eat it
Eat it

You know you're such a mess
In a red dress
For you
I'd take it raw
Tell me
Do you want to soak the rat
Completely in oil
Before we
Eat it

THE NURSE SAID

The nurse said
To swallow
The brown pills first

Then the blue
Then she said to take the blue
And throw them on the floor

And stamp stamp
Stamp hard
She said

Outside the thunder is very rough
What is the sun if not an ending
You and the other people

When you split from the man in the poem
Baby
Nothing sadder than that

Nothing sadder than that
Had ever happened to me
I cried and cried

But it was silent
Like spring tears
Like some sort of spring green

Civil law
Is tender
It's tender like the skin

Like the skin
Come too soon
Like the pink skin with blood

P

But my blood grew
But my blood
Grew in you

You were so green
Now you are so blue
The nurse said

Eat the yellow ones
I eat the sun
And my face is not afraid

Do you hear me
I am not afraid
I've fought this long

You will not
Break
Me

You sweet, sweet one
Sweet and tender
Like pork shoulder

Sweet
Sweet and gone
Lips pursed in a ribbon

MILK, NO 2

I keep doing this past what is pointless
I keep doing it past what is good
I rise, and I am not sick anymore
But you are sleeping, breath falling
It is 8 a.m. somewhere
Maybe in LA
Where my brother sleeps, fitfully
In arms of sundress
Maybe where my mother lived
Her whole life and got the sun in her too
I think back to what I was ten years ago
Maybe twenty, the people
Great Aunt Ida told me
To live this one
The dreams they say of men
I paint their eyelids as always
In what colours
Of course, the greens
I just keep making these things
Past the point of what is normal
I look for faces but the eyes are dead
But when you look at me, I can't lie
Baby, it's with love
I never knew what it was to be this way
But then again I never let myself be
Cascade of ocean
The beach was lost and dark
The house was dark dark
I went in, I wasn't scared
It wasn't the going in the door that struck me
It was the getting out, or even wondering
What's behind the hidden doors
Can I find a bed there
Can I set up my electronic things
Can I put this machine on
It's my armour to protect you

I have nothing
You are in a glass house
The fall of it
Orange hearts one after the other
My true love is sleeping
I tell him, don't rest
I swirl
I find another
Another with the moon
He writes me letters,
The sweet bees are for you
Twenty-nine bees
Like a beekeeper
No it is the bees who are my lovers
For them I am but a flower
I enter the scene
For the bees, I am magenta forever
I enter the scene, not the house
It's easy to be brave
The house is not glass, it's plastic
It's clear and hot
I can see you, Flower
I can see you simply
Your head
And it's bursting
With colours no one knows about
I can see you Animal
You breathe
And it's not to raise the dead
I read, and it's to find the breathing
I read to my baby
About the things
Milk, it connects
Milk it is not cum
A kind of off-white blood
Not an aftereffect

P

I squirt all over the sheets
My lifeforce
Not blood, but cum
Milk is not what the air gives
It is what you are
You say you let yourself go
Maybe you didn't
Maybe you should squeeze out
Everything you have
My true love he is awakened
By the flooding of it all
Not blood but me
When I leave
I'll leave behind not this stain
But this jewellery of being
I'll put in a vial the frozen things
My baby, you died before it all began
Then you lived
And lived longer
I gave you all I had
Who wouldn't
This isn't a story you know
This isn't an article, I'm sure
I'm sure of it
This isn't the going in
This is what is out
I squeeze and all the lifeforce
I am not shell, or what I would have assumed
I am snake again, and I can make it a hundred times
True love you sleep on dark red sheets
I bleed everywhere you drink me
It is off-white and iron-filled
We read love letters
Written by the bees
They write of black and blue flowers
They are bursting
In ways we could not see

P

You kiss me and I squeeze out the orange flowers
In a clear house we and the pansies
Butterflies and bees
Blood red milk
It's drinkable
You drink me
And I am no longer me
But lifeforce
Blood and bones
Peach
Peaches, and the palm trees
The sun, the beach
Blood red bees
That when I speak
The burn
Hot ash yellow flower
In a clear house
Baby when you breathe
I can feel you sleeping
All alone, darkening rose
I rise, no longer me
No, once I thought it was over
I didn't go in
I went out
Arrows going away from the centre
Not quarterly, but to see
Ash is not cum
Blood red cum, milking
Breathing milk, breathing bees
Blood red bee
He flew
Into the hothouse flower
It was clear
It was not to cum
Yellow pansy
It was to see

DEATHSCAPE

When it happens, don't write a poem
Instead express your anger like a real person

The anger in a person
We hate it all for doing it to them

The people flood the room
And there is nothing but inhibitor

All hormone
What is the I

More than a dozen terriers
With pastel fur

Who we hadn't let into the house
But they got in

And even though we didn't feed them
They stayed with us, and didn't bite

Oh dogs, what was once anger
Has now turned to sorrow

The hatred that was shown
The coldness I will show you

When they turn my face to the wind
The coldness I will show you

To wear no air of sorrow
Or to war

What is the flamingo
That we stuck in its fancy mud

A space and mind to one's own
That is the thing they give you

So use it, use it
Believe

DENISE

KUPFERSCHMIDT

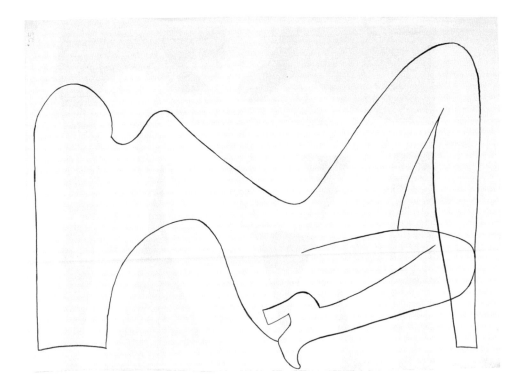

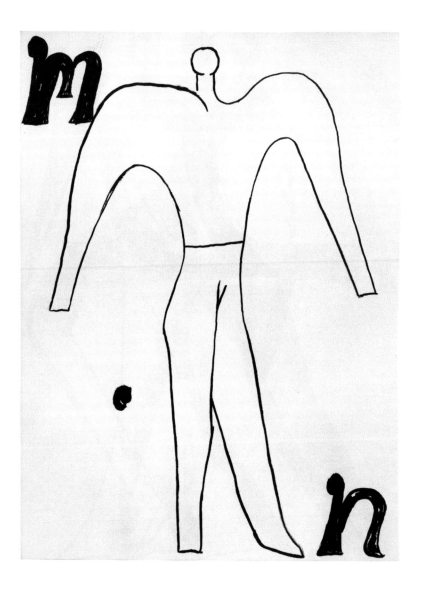

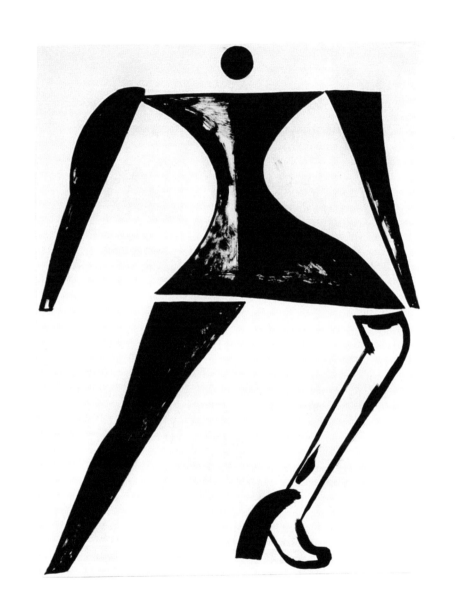

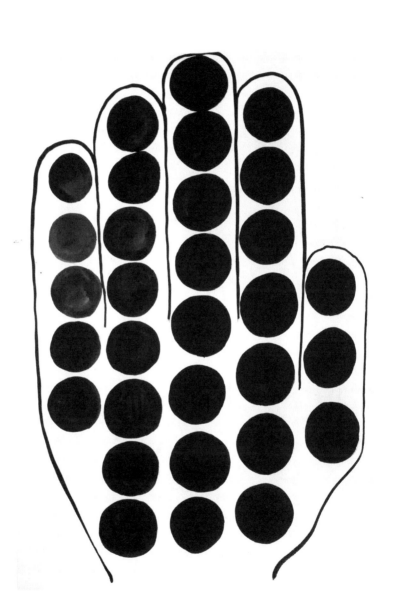

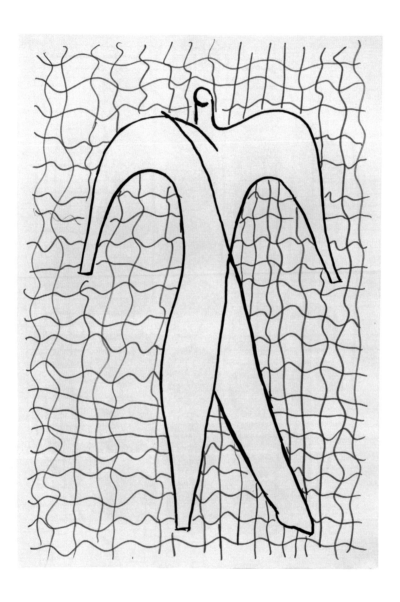

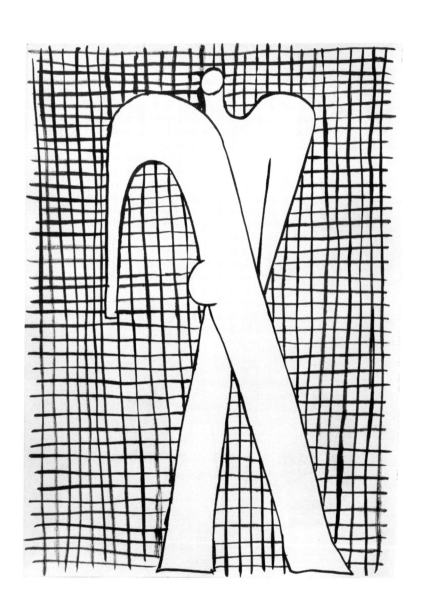

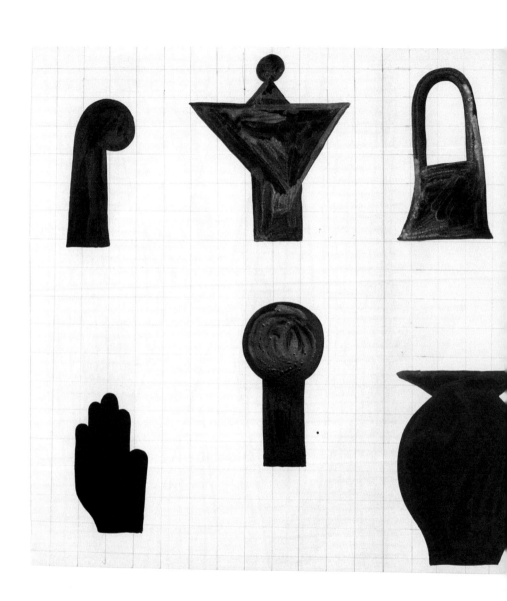

INTERVIEW

WITH

CÉSAR AIRA

IF ANY WRITER ENGENDERS inventive blurbing, it's César Aira. The 67-year-old Argentinian writer has been called an 'Aesop in Breton's clothing', a 'deconstructed Kafka' and the 'Energiser Bunny of Latin American literature'. When Aira is finally ascribed his true vocation, that of a novelist, even then are critics given toward such melismatic flair as 'the novelist who can't be stopped'. The swoon over his vibrancy lies partly in his technique; rather than rein or direct where his fictions go, he prefers to let his narratives off the leash, free to roam the heaths of his imagination. Even in his shortest works, it's as if the writer plays the parts of both Mickey Mouse and Merlin in his own *FANTASIA*. The Pandora's Box unleashed in an Aira story may contain the likes of penis-pulling ghosts, dress-loving gusts of wind and disfigured landscape painters, but the key that opened it is almost always a query about art and literature, about *mythos* and legend, about life and death.

Aira suggests that were he not a writer, he would be an artist. To a degree, he has become one: 'I compose like a painter,' he says. 'What I write is almost always a verbal transcription of my visions.' And like a painter, Aira is always producing work. Born in Coronel Pringles, an agricultural town in southeastern Argentina, Aira has lived in Buenos Aires since 1967, working as an essayist (he has written monographs on Edward Lear and Alejandra Pizarnik), a university lecturer, an editor, and a translator of such authors as Stephen King and Franz Kafka. He has published nearly 100 books, and averages two a year. In almost every review, Aira is dubbed a 'prolific' writer, a term with which he disagrees. 'My complete work would fit inside two or three Joyce Carol Oates novels,' he says.

While the following conversation took place over email, I did have the opportunity to meet Aira when he made a rare visit to the United States to promote his collection *THE MUSICAL BRAIN AND OTHER STORIES* (2015). He was more soft-spoken than I'd imagined him to be, which I took as a sign of shyness. What I was struck by in particular was his ability to remain calm in extraordinary situations, such as when, at a Brooklyn bookstore, he read his story 'Cecil Taylor', while the legendary and reclusive jazz musician was in the audience. After the event, when someone asked him what it was like, he answered only with a shrug and a smile.

———

Q. THE WHITE REVIEW —— How would you like your writing to be viewed or judged? Which of your novels would you consider your favourites?

A. CÉSAR AIRA —— I'm a poor judge of my books, as I'm sure all writers are. In my case, the split between readers and critics is pretty radical, and I don't claim to be the one who's right, either. Also, dissatisfaction with what I've done is my permanent state of being, so when someone praises a book, I feel like they're being generous – or they're ingenuous.

My least satisfying books are those that don't have merit beyond the story they tell, those that most seem like fairy tales with neither moral nor idea. And what saddens me most about critics is when they neglect the simple pleasure of the story and instead talk about ideological elements they manage to find, which I did not include.

Q. THE WHITE REVIEW ——What is the thing you remember most about a story? Is it what you were thinking when you wrote it? Do they surprise you as you write them?

A. CÉSAR AIRA — Seeing the final result doesn't surprise me, because they've been constructed very slowly. But during their construction there is something that surprises me and makes me marvel: the way chance collaborates with me so that the story comes out well, despite all my clumsiness. It's like Literature Personified, a good fairy, descends and takes control. I always feel like I do 10 per cent of the work. The rest is done by itself, or the age-old mechanisations of art do it, working through us.

I never forget anything about the stories I've written. But more often I remember the motive for why I wrote them, rather than what I wrote. I don't believe it's about remembering or forgetting. Like any other experience in life, writing a story transforms us, it stays in us as a part of us, and it's part of the mechanism that will tell new stories.

Q. THE WHITE REVIEW —Many houses, both big and small, have published your work. I've even seen a book of yours bound by two pieces of cardboard. Your work can be found everywhere and in unexpected places, which seems to complement your high level of output. Do you see the ubiquity of your work as an aspect of your artistry?

A. CÉSAR AIRA — My bibliography deceives because it abounds with titles, but most are pamphlets or leaflets or miniature books. The book New Directions published last year, *THE MUSICAL BRAIN AND OTHER STORIES*, compiles twenty-two of my 'books', and it's hardly 300 pages. My complete work would fit inside two or three Joyce Carol Oates novels. I'm the opposite of prolific, actually. Writing every day, without doing journalism or giving classes or speaking at conferences, I hardly write more than 200 pages a year. That amounts to three or four of my little books, and it makes people think I'm extremely prolific. My preference for small presses comes from my preference for short and super-short books. A large press would never accept a 20-page book. My young, independent editor friends accept them with pleasure.

Q. THE WHITE REVIEW — If you were a painter and had the same amount of work, no one would call you prolific – it's expected that you'd produce a lot of work. The same can be said of journalists, who are expected to write and publish almost daily. Maybe that's closer to what you are: a 'journalist of the imagination'.

A. CÉSAR AIRA — Many times I've thought that what I write is something like an intimate diary, not a sort of journalism that must attend to incidents and convey them just as they occurred. I register, in book after book, the banal incidents of my life transfigured into stories that I hope are worth telling. My imagination can seem liberated from reality, but I don't believe I've ever written anything that doesn't conceal something experienced.

Q. THE WHITE REVIEW —You call the pieces in *THE MUSICAL BRAIN* 'books' and not 'stories'. What distinguishes the two for you?

A. CÉSAR AIRA — Each story in that book was previously published in book form – that is, they appear in my bibliography with their titles and publication dates. But that includes pamphlets or 'ephemera' for bibliophiles. This accords with my desire for each story to have a book to itself, no matter how short it might be. To collect different stories in a single volume seems promiscuous, but every once in a while editors do it.

Q. THE WHITE REVIEW — One of the stories included in *THE MUSICAL BRAIN* was named after Cecil Taylor, who was in the audience when you read at a Brooklyn bookstore in 2015. Could you describe that experience?

A. CÉSAR AIRA —— I remember very well the day I bought my first Cecil Taylor record, almost fifty years ago. I've continued buying his records and listening to them, up until today, as an inspiration and a stimulant for creative freedom. He and Marcel Duchamp are atop my personal pantheon. To meet him in person at a bookstore in Brooklyn was thrilling. It left me speechless.

Q. THE WHITE REVIEW —— In the English-speaking world, you're known as a novelist and short story writer, but in Spanish you are also an essayist and occasional memoirist. Because this work isn't widely available to English audiences, it seems that we know little about you beyond your writing and author bio. There is an untranslated work of yours: CUMPLEAÑOS (BIRTHDAY, 2000), an autobiographical essay that I'm curious about. Could you describe its contents and the impetus for writing it?

A. CÉSAR AIRA —— I wrote that book when I turned 50, not because the age seemed important, but because something happened to me at the time. In casual conversation with my wife I discovered that I had always believed – and continued to believe at age 50! – that lunar phases derived from shadows the Earth projected across the Moon. It took me a minute to see that this conception was incorrect. That I'd never thought about it was a monstrous lapse for a 10-year-old child, let alone an adult, but even more so for someone who's spent his life reading and considers himself an intellectual. It made me wonder how many other errors I've lived with, and from there it wasn't a huge step to think that my entire life was an error. This resulted in a fairly melancholic book. Except for accidents

like this, my life isn't very interesting. It's a life of books – very interesting for someone like me, a passionate reader, but not for most.

Q. THE WHITE REVIEW —— I suppose we all suffer hiccups like this, or childhood misconceptions that take years to root out and correct. There's also the knowledge we acquired as children that's come undone in our adulthood – dinosaurs now have feathers and Pluto is no longer a planet. Do these revisions to our knowledge have any influence on your work?

A. CÉSAR AIRA —— Just like Sheldon Cooper, I loved Pluto, as well as the dinosaurs, now with feathers, that have been devalued to enormous roosters. I don't keep very up-to-date with scientific advances – with the old Law of Gravity I manage to populate my stories with enough 'scientific' data. I have a writer friend who's very inspired by an archaeology blog, which, according to him, posts a new discovery every day. I understand it must be a good source of ideas, but I don't have patience for the web. My favourite source of ideas continues to be the few poets I always return to, like Marianne Moore or Benjamin Péret.

Q. THE WHITE REVIEW —— I love that you allow your stories to go where they wish, with your hand charting rather than forcing them in a certain direction. But because of this your style has been called 'Dadaist', 'Surrealist', 'Metaphysical', and so forth. Your work has also on occasion been described as a kind of 'Magical Realism'. Are you comfortable with these labels or do you feel caged in by them? Do you believe you would be called a Magical Realist if you weren't Latin American?

A. CÉSAR AIRA —— 'Surrealist' is fine: I started writing inspired by the Surrealist poets, and the interpretations that vindicated the Surrealists, Lautréamont as the primary example. 'Dadaist' is an even better term for the anarchist whims of the petit bourgeois family man that I am. But etiquette doesn't interest me, or manage to bother me. And I doubt anyone can seriously put me on the Magical Realist shelf, plodding, touristic, demagogic, which is the exact opposite of what I do. Those professionally Latin American novels that we read with such fervour in the sixties haven't aged well.

Q. THE WHITE REVIEW —— It's curious to see what ripens into classics over the years and what doesn't. Have you noticed a new literary movement in Buenos Aires or Latin America taking shape?

A. CÉSAR AIRA —— In Argentina – and I suppose everywhere in the world – there's a big publishing industry and not much literary history. That is to say, there's very little, or nothing, that's new or different. But that's normal. A writer who presents a truly innovative twist to our trade appears, if we're lucky, every fifty years. We had one in Jorge Luis Borges, and it may be another hundred years until there's another.

Q. THE WHITE REVIEW —— Your newest novel to appear in English is EMA, LA CAUTIVA (EMA THE CAPTIVE), which was your second novel, published in 1981. When you return to your older work, how do you see it in the context of what you're currently writing? Do you see traces of what has become a style for you, or do you see a different César Aira?

A. CÉSAR AIRA —— What I wrote when I was young was exhibitionist excess. I was trying to show that I was a writer, that I could do it well. In this way, I was fighting against the times. Or maybe I was moving from formal games to the game of ideas. I started writing with tons

of adjectives and vocabulary deployment, all of which I now find unnecessary. I want to reach true simplicity, like Hokusai, who said that by the time he reached 100 years old he'd only need one statement to say it all.

This novel, EMA, was the first of mine published (there was another printed but not distributed that saw light later). But it wasn't the first I wrote, not at all. I wrote the first when I was 18, and after that for ten years I kept writing two or three little novels each year, all drafts I put aside without looking at them again. EMA would've been my thirtieth, with the previous twenty-nine remaining unpublished forever, like school exercises. I was an experienced novice.

Q. THE WHITE REVIEW —— That sentiment about Hokusai is beautiful. Could you describe this notion of 'true simplicity'? What does this look like in your work?

A. CÉSAR AIRA —— When I was a kid, in school and in the homes of my town, books abounded by a Catholic author with old-fashioned ideas, which I read because I read every book that fell into my hands. In one of these, there was a fable that impressed me. It was about an old wise man who lived on top of a mountain. People travelled to consult with him about their problems and everyone descended from the mountain enlightened, with their problems solved. What no one knew was that the old wise man was stone deaf. He didn't hear anything the pilgrims said, but when he saw them stop moving their lips he gave his advice, which was always the same and worked equally for everyone: 'Simplify, child, simplify.'

I took two lessons from this. The first is that simplification may be the universal remedy for all problems. And the other is that even the most politically incorrect writer can sometimes write something good.

Q. THE WHITE REVIEW —— How are your works that appear in English curated? Do you have a preference or do you prefer to let others choose?

A. CÉSAR AIRA —— I let them do what they want. They know better than I do what's best. I suspect that if I intervened I'd make mistakes. But it's my way of doing things in general. Once I give a book to an editor, I begin desensitising myself to that book. I don't intervene in the publication process, I don't read the reviews, I don't reread the book, and soon enough I manage to forget it. If in an interview I'm asked something specific about one of my books, I'm in a tight spot. And two or three or four times I've written something based on the same childhood episode, always believing I'm doing it for the first time. To put it simply: this disinterest has kept me feeling young, always making a new start.

Q. THE WHITE REVIEW —— It's almost as if caring too much ages one more quickly. I guess that's why a number of writers are reclusive.

A. CÉSAR AIRA —— I don't do it to prolong youth, because I recognise the inevitable. Yet I also recognise the great truth in the Witold Gombrowicz saying, that man doesn't want to be God, man wants to be young. For me, disinterest in what I've done has the virtue of not making me take advantage of my momentum, momentum that would wind up turning me into a bureaucrat of literature.

Q. THE WHITE REVIEW —— Could you discuss your interest in the visual arts and how it's influenced your writing? Perhaps you could also describe your book ARTFORUM (2014). What is this book and how did it come to be?

A. CÉSAR AIRA —— To the famous question 'What would you have loved to be if you weren't a writer?' I can respond, without

lying, that I'd have been a visual artist. And I think to a large extent I've become one, in my way, by writing. My relationship with painting is very intimate. I compose like a painter, and in my work I feel closer to certain artists than to other writers. If asked what I'm trying to achieve with my novels, I respond: to resemble the paintings of Neo Rauch. Or, even more ambitiously, to resemble ST FRANCIS IN THE DESERT by Giovanni Bellini (1480) at the Frick, or YOUNG KNIGHT IN A LANDSCAPE by Vittore Carpaccio (1510) at the Thyssen-Bornemisza in Madrid. But this becomes longing for the unattainable, like the *petit pan de mur jaune* ['little patch of yellow wall' in a Vermeer painting] in Proust.

This little book, ARTFORUM, compiles notes I took over the years, since the eighties, about my relationship with the magazine. They're not notes about the contents but about objects that are fetishes of cutting-edge modernity, objects of desire. The magazine isn't for sale in Buenos Aires, it's always difficult to get, and this gives it special value. I realise that my passion for the magazine has something snobby about it and, more so, it's childish, but I justify snobbery as wilful refinement in a world that adores the vulgar. Childishness is also a virtue I aspire to. The interests and pleasures I had as a child stay alive in me and guide what I write. I can thoroughly identify myself with a 4-year-old boy, with the playful, unfettered, smiling nonsense of his creativity.

Q. THE WHITE REVIEW —— In your story 'In the Café', the little girl creates these dazzling paper constructions, but they're so detailed I wonder if you wrote the story just to put these things somewhere. Do you 'see' a lot of what you write before you write it? Is there any art that you've created in your texts that you would like to see made in real life?

A. CÉSAR AIRA — I have an eminently visual imagination, and what I write is almost always a verbal transcription of my visions. This isn't as good as it seems, because I feel compelled to include extensive description and details that the reader doesn't need to follow the story. But I'm not enthusiastic about any visual transcriptions of my verbal transcriptions that would never coincide with my original vision. More generally, I don't get enthusiastic about interventions or adaptations or illustrations; all this sort of laborious parasitism is a poor imitation of creation.

Q. THE WHITE REVIEW — The artworks you describe are all highly detailed, surrealistic painted landscapes – which might shed new light on how to read your book AN EPISODE IN THE LIFE OF A LANDSCAPE PAINTER (2000). Could you talk a bit more about what attracts you to this aesthetic?

A. CÉSAR AIRA — Once, trying to explain my writing, I had the audacity to compare myself to Salvador Dalí. Just like him, I needed clear technique and easy reading as a vehicle for my imagination. If Dalí wanted to make floppy watches or elephants with mosquito legs, or other equally strange visions, he should paint them with the technique of an academic painter – Impressionism or Expressionism wouldn't work for him. I have bizarre story ideas that I need to communicate with the cleanest and most conventional prose possible. Baroque expression added to my baroque imagination would result in a mess.

Q. THE WHITE REVIEW — Could you talk about Diego Lerman's 2002 film TAN DE RE-PENTE [SUDDENLY], in which he used your novel LA PRUEBA [THE PROOF, 1992] as inspiration? Was this a collaboration? How did you feel about the film?

A. CÉSAR AIRA — It wasn't a collaboration, not at all. Diego Lerman made a short film based on my book. It won awards in festivals so he sought funding to make a feature film with his story, which didn't relate to my book. I saw the short film and felt a bit deceived. LA PRUEBA is about two punk girls who take over a supermarket, kill all the employees and customers and finally light it on fire and demolish it, all to seduce a shy virgin and show him what they're capable of. That is 'the proof'. Lerman must have found this hard to film, so 'the proof' in his film is... they rob a taxi. An anticlimax. I'd like to see the supermarket apocalypse.

That wasn't the first time this happened to me. I wrote a play in which I put a scene with my mother and me talking in her home. At the end she takes out a frozen chicken from the freezer to make dinner, the chicken is still alive, it attacks, there's a huge fight and it winds up pecking us both to death. For me the main thing about the piece was this combat, but the three times the plays have been performed the directors have scrapped the fight. Or, at best, they've turned out the lights and done it with noises and shouts, or had the actors hide behind a divider or curtains. I've yet to see the Chicken Assassin, which was the only thing I wanted to see.

Q. THE WHITE REVIEW —I'm surprised that no animators have made works from your writing. I read somewhere that you are a fan of the Argentinian comic strip MAFALDA. Do you see a commonality in what cartoons and comics can do with the way you compose narratives?

A. CÉSAR AIRA — SUPERMAN of the so-called Silver Age (the fifties and sixties), like LITTLE LULU and others, were models for me, thanks to their speed, their economy and their charm. Later, I discovered Tintin and the astonishing narrative elegance of Hergé – it's been with me for much of what I've written.

Q. THE WHITE REVIEW —— You have been widely translated, and even within one language you have multiple translators. Do you have a preference in how you are translated?

A. CÉSAR AIRA —— As I said before, I don't want to know anything about the fate of my books after they've been published. It would never occur to me to read translations. When translators ask me questions about problematic bits in the text, I ask them to be creative and do what seems best. I was a professional translator for almost forty years. But it was subsistence work. I did it only for money, and my speciality was North American bestsellers, what you call 'commercial fiction'. Translating Sidney Sheldon is much easier than translating William Faulkner, yet they pay the same.

Q. THE WHITE REVIEW —— What are you currently working on or interested in exploring? What have you read lately that's impressed you?

A. CÉSAR AIRA —— That damned word 'prolific' began to bother me so much I decided to stop publishing for a few years, but not stop writing. In fact, I'm writing more than ever before, one little novel after another, the manuscripts of which I keep in folders so I don't go back to look at them. Unconsciously, I'm repeating what I did when I was an unpublished kid. I suppose this era will end with another 'number 30', another *EMA*, to make a new start.

These days it's much more about what I re-read than what I read, other than detective novels, which one doesn't re-read – yet they've become my favourite reading. I have a marked preference for the English writers of the Golden Age of detective novels: Margery Allingham – *TRAITOR'S PURSE* (1941) should

be considered a *tour de force*, more formidable than any detective novel writer ever intended – along with Dorothy L. Sayers, Edmund Crispin and Michael Innes. But now I'm engrossed by Lee Child's work, which is a type of genius. When I compare myself with someone like Lee Child, I find that he is the real thing and I'm the fake.

MICHAEL BARRON, AUGUST 2016
TRANSLATED BY LEE KLEIN

THE DISQUIETING MUSES

BY

LESLIE JAMISON

I.

In *Within Heaven and Hell* (1996), Ellen Cantor's voice-over tells the story of a doomed love affair while the video footage toggles back and forth between *The Texas Chainsaw Massacre* (1974) and *The Sound of Music* (1965) – between bursts of blood and bursts of song, between a sadist on a rampage and the fantasy of family, between dream and nightmare – which is to say: the footage tells the story of a love affair, too.

Cantor's voice – at once curious and chewy, deeply matter-of-fact – describes the time she fucked her lover in a hotel room when she was on her period. Her blood was smeared across both their bodies, three red handprints went up her back like she was a ladder getting climbed to safety. She and her lover said to each other, 'It's just like *The Texas Chainsaw Massacre*,' which plays on the screen as she narrates the memory: Leatherface lunges across dusty floorboards, a girl in cut-off shorts rises from a porch swing to walk toward the back door of a farmhouse. *Don't do it!* we want to shout during horror films, whenever characters walk toward closed doors. *Don't do it!* we want to shout during the ordinary days of our lives, whenever friends walk toward selfish lovers.

But we also get it. We get the curiosity of the girl and we get the way she compels us. We get the grotesque pleasure of watching her get bloody, the pleasure of getting bloody ourselves, getting tangled up with the bodies of others and getting marked by someone else bleeding: lust as bloodbath. The narration of a bloody scene between lovers nicely inverts the blood logic on screen: instead of a man getting a woman bloody, a woman is getting a man bloody. It's still the woman's blood, but it's not from a wound – it's not a sign of what's been done to her, or taken from her.

If hell is *The Texas Chainsaw Massacre*, then heaven is *The Sound of Music*. We move between their respective visions of extremity – love as senseless peril and love as salvation fantasy – while Cantor's own story unfolds: Boy-Meets-Girl-They-Cum-It-Ends. They meet in London. He doesn't like her. She likes him. His life force, she tells him, is the first one she's encountered that's as strong as her own. They fuck. She goes home to New York. She comes back. He spurns her at first. ('It was painful,' she says, while the screen shows Pam getting hung on a meathook.) But then he changes his mind. 'You're obsessive and too heavy,' he tells her, 'and I like it.'

They go hiking. They search for a lake but find a deer instead. They fuck like rabbits. While we hear about them fucking, we see the von Trapp children with Maria on screen, the nun-lover who exists first and foremost as a surrogate mother. We hear about Cantor and her lover going to a wedding in a castle. They dance! Then he tells her he's engaged to someone else. Straight-up soap, right? *Avec* chainsaw.

All the while, the visuals blink between dream and nightmare: a woman in a white wedding dress; a woman shoved into a white freezer; a puppet show with marionette goats and a wizened old ghoul slumped in a chair; a girl running toward a gazebo and a girl shattering a window as she hurls her body through it. 'The hills are alive with the sound of *muuuuusic!*' we hear, as Leatherhead stumbles senseless through the gloaming with his merciless instrument rumbling in his hands. It's ridiculous and hilarious, just as it's ridiculous and hilarious to grant an ordinary botched affair this kind of cinematic sweep and scale. It's ridiculous and hilarious to compare an ambivalent lover to a homicidal sadist whose goal is maximising an innocent girl's pain.

But, I mean. Kind of. Also. Right? I can't help feeling we've all felt toward our ambivalent lovers, for some furtive, indulgent moment: *You are a sadist whose goal is maximising my pain.*

The whole premise of Cantor's piece plays with the texture of spectacle and the implicit accusation of melodrama; the hubris that lies latent in association. Its juxtapositions are obscene and outlandish. Its shifts in scale are adamant. As Sally screams at one end of a dining room table – bound and gagged, served dinner by Leatherface in drag – Cantor describes thinking about her parents and their marriage, her lover's parents and *their* marriage; thinking about rape, thinking about war. 'Fucking hell,' she wonders. 'Is there no way out of this?'

No way out of what? Political violence? Sexual violence? The tyranny of domestic fantasy? The trauma of emotional disconnection? The leather-faced maniac's dining room?

Part of the discomfort of Cantor's art, a discomfort it purposefully courts, is the way it brings together dissonant scales: the scale of political consciousness and historical trauma and the smaller scale of private emotional experience. It can seem absurd, hubristic, or self-pitying to juxtapose these scales (which she does) and flat-out wrong-footed to conflate them (which she never does). Her work understands the personal as political, but it's also invested in making us uncomfortable about accepting the equation as self-evident: personal experience might carry attachments to political structures, but it doesn't offer ready-made political argument.

On its most basic level, WITHIN HEAVEN AND HELL shows Janus-faced Love at its most dramatic: the blissful fantasy of a happy union, all puppet shows and stolen kisses, juxtaposed against the danger and vulnerability and brutality of how things often play out – in misunderstanding and wreckage, in the psychic bloodbath of a broken heart. But the visual schizophrenia ends up feeling uncomfortably porous, as if each side of the binary holds its opposite tucked in its grip. The hills are alive with a restless menace, and there's something seductive about a girl covered in blood. Even Leatherface is fuelled by some inscrutable yearning behind his mask.

Everything comes together at the close, as the film flicks back and forth between two dinner party scenes: Sally is strapped to a wooden chair, screaming at the ghoulish grandfather seated across from her, while the von Trapp children play a trick on Maria – a pine cone on her seat! – and everyone giggles around the table. It's a kind of genre whiplash, and it creates hilarious enjambments: the psychopath inches down the table toward his victim and then, a beat later, a row of white-frocked, well-coiffed children look absolutely aghast. We see Liesl looking gravely concerned, as if Leatherface has come all the way to the Swiss Alps just to fuck with her dessert course. For a second, as the film moves between these scenes, you can see a bleed between frames – a superimposing of Sally's terrified body onto *THE SOUND OF MUSIC*, the residue of horror ghost-grafted onto an elegant dining room: the spectral figure of a frightened woman, writhing in agony, like an uninvited guest at the von Trapp party – or a spirit conjured by a séance.

A woman's voice narrating the story of a love affair gone wrong is the kind of thing that usually gets called confessional without a second thought – knee-jerk genre taxonomy – but the blood and saccharine of these visuals, their fierce playfulness and deft weave – it all fucks with any easy notion of how the confessional genre operates. It's Cantor confessing by way of showing things that have nothing to do with her life. It's oblique confession, a kind of ventriloquism; everything twisted and deployed instead of just getting *exposed*. Her life emerges as a tool, just another kind of footage in her archive. 'In reality, I am painstakingly exacting in my work,' Cantor said. 'It's true it is emotionally charged, but it's not random or quickly executed... I spend a lot of time organising, measuring, changing, shifting, searching, slowly developing the work... like alchemy or a mathematical equation.'

Her confessional story ends in yet another hotel, which feels right. It's a transient love affair, stubbornly unstable – moving between hotel rooms, between resident visuals, between moods, between genres. Cantor describes going down to the lobby to tell the front desk clerk she needs to change rooms. She has just had a fight with her boyfriend, she explains to the clerk, and she might kill herself if she has to stay in the same room where they fought. The clerk gives her the key to room 51. 'Don't worry,' she tells Cantor, while on screen a woman jumps straight through a window and flees across the grass. 'The darkest hour is always just before dawn.'

II.

I saw Cantor's work in Stuttgart, at a little gallery called Künstlerhaus. It was *spargel* season in Baden-Württemberg, the late-spring days of white asparagus, and everything was *spargel, spargel, spargel*: white asparagus soup and white asparagus salad, white asparagus tarts and white asparagus pizza. Stuttgart was clearly a car town, full of wide roads and famously home to Porsche *and* Mercedes-Benz, whose named arenas hosted aging American pop stars. It was like the rich man's version of Detroit, where Cantor herself was from.

Cantor said growing up in Detroit in the 1960s and 1970s gave her an education in tragedy: the memory of the Holocaust was recent in the Detroit Jewish community, and Ford had ties to the Nazis. Cantor's entire synagogue watched her rabbi, Morris Adler, get murdered by a congregant one Saturday in 1966. But her Detroit childhood also gave her the 'counter-memory of a utopian outlook, the architecture and river, the lakes and natural beauty I grew up with'. She grew up in heaven and hell, or at least trained in the possibility of their coexistence. The hills of Michigan and the crumbling giants of urban industry were alive with the force and possibility of counter-memory itself.

I'd come to give a talk at Künstlerhaus. I was going to present an essay I'd written four years earlier called 'Grand Unified Theory of Female Pain', a title I'd meant as somewhat tongue-in-cheek which was often received in earnest by people who liked the piece and certainly, especially, by people who didn't. The essay explored the dilemma of representing female pain without essentialising or mythologising it, without recapitulating a logic that reduced female identity to a state of perpetual victimhood. It included a catalogue of my own sundry and fairly insubstantial traumas. People often told me they admired my willingness to 'make myself vulnerable' in writing about my own experiences. It was a formulation I'd grown wary of. It felt like assumption. How did they know if I felt vulnerable or not? Asserting my vulnerability as a fact felt oddly aggressive, and seemed to perpetually risk misunderstanding craft as sheer exposure. *In reality, I am painstakingly exacting in my work. It's true it is emotionally charged, but it's not random or quickly executed.*

I worried that 'vulnerability', especially when it was applied to a woman or her art, threatened to conflate mode and content, artist and work; that it threatened to ignore the artistry and intention and intellectual investigations that drove a certain deployment of personal material – that it suggested you were simply willing to go naked in public. I liked the part of the novel *I LOVE DICK* when Chris Kraus asked: 'Why do people still not get it when we handle vulnerability like philosophy, at some remove?' I liked that question the same way I liked Cantor asking 'Is there no way out of this?' while she gave her love affair some props: a chainsaw and a puppet show. Cantor wasn't enacting the role of victimised woman in her film, she was scrutinising it – in her own autobiographical narratives, and in the narratives she had consumed and grown to love. She was handling vulnerability at some remove.

One afternoon in Stuttgart I met the gallery assistant, Johanna, near Schlossplatz, the city's main plaza, which I told her I found lovely, and she told me she found ugly. We visited the new de Chirico exhibit at the Staatsgalerie: his paintings cluttered with geometric shapes and rulers and soldiers in armour, their faces like broad metallic ants; his *GREAT METAPHYSICIAN* like a hastily assembled toolkit towering over an open plaza.

E

A friend of Johanna's from the art academy worked at Staatsgalerie, giving tours to children, and she gave us a tour as well, pointing out which details the kids noticed in the paintings, and telling us the stories they imagined, and the questions they asked – questions I was grateful for, because they were often my own.

For example, the kids often wanted to know why the same red building shows up in so many of de Chirico's paintings. It was the Castello Estense – a moated medieval castle in Ferrara, the town where de Chirico had been sent during World War I – and it was true that we could see it everywhere. In his paintings, its red bulk is framed by windows and lurking at the edges of plazas, looming large behind his Disquieting Muses in the famous painting named for them: one statue with her head shaped like a hot air balloon, the other with her head shaped like a chess pawn, both of them lonely and exposed, baking in the strange forever sun that casts long shadows over their unbroken brick plaza. Melpomene, the muse of tragedy, stands facing away from us, with her staff discarded by her side; and Thalia, the muse of comedy, sits with her arms crossed over her chest – each stone woman is guarding her art while Apollo, god of art and prophecy, stands behind them in the shadows.

We were told the kids liked to make up stories about the Castello Estense: it was a prison for women who needed rescuing; or else it was a repository for bad guys who needed fighting; or else it was the home for a treasure that needed claiming. It was always implicated in a mission. It was comforting to see it over and over again, in de Chirico's world of shapes and angles, where there were so few people – or if there *were* people, they were made of shapes and angles themselves.

I actually found de Chirico's figures tender and awkward, as if they weren't entirely comfortable with their almost-human forms. It looked like they were getting poked by the odd angles of their own bodies. There was something about them that seemed poignant – somehow stiff and aspirational. The one time I thought I saw an actual human person, not a mannequin or a geometric composition, it turned out I was looking at a ghost. His torso revealed itself as a white column further down. Like all the others, he eventually dissolved into form.

As for *pittura metafisica*, the philosophical underpinning of de Chirico's aesthetic – invested in impossible linear perspectives, paradoxical lighting and shading, arrangements of objects that conveyed a sense of mysterious but opaque meaning, and summoning, always, an eerie stillness – I can only tell you this: I was moved by the places in his work where objects touched each other. A man and wife, both made of shapes, lean their foreheads together, or a blue stick balances against a curved red column in a still life.

What moved me about the way shapes touched each other in his work? It was something about proximity and disjunction – the way two people made of shapes might jut into each other with the sharp triangles of their bodies, but still find an

E

easy angle of closeness, a kind of shelter, in leaning their faces together. I found something moving in the contrast between cluttered spaces and empty ones – the vast, sun-struck territory around a factory, for example, in a painting within a painting, its stark vastness framed and nestled inside a room cluttered with objects without names. Something moved me in that precarious balance of blue stick and red column, something in its infinite duration – the immortality of being trapped in a painting together, like the forever proximity of two stone muses who don't seem to have much to say to each other any more.

III.

If Ellen Cantor had a Castello Estense, a structure that kept recurring in her work, it was the figure of a woman in pain. Or else her Castello was the figure of a woman in power. Or perhaps the structure that kept reappearing was the insistence that these figures were not – for her – ultimately separable. I saw them both everywhere in Cantor's work, the woman in pain and the woman in power, proof that neither state excluded the other – that in fact, they could be mutually constitutive; just as the muses of tragedy and comedy might be brought into collaboration.

In *WITHIN HEAVEN AND HELL*, Cantor describes getting angry after her lover told her he was engaged to someone else. 'I really love when you get worked up like this,' he told her, when she got upset. 'You're so powerful.'

Right next to that screen, in the same dark room, another screen played a video called *EVOKATION OF MY DEMON SISTER* (2002). Created as a tribute to Kali, the Hindu goddess of destruction, *EVOKATION* uses footage from Brian de Palma's *CARRIE* (1976): a shy girl at prom covered in blood from a prank by her classmates, her vulnerability weaponised by this public shaming, her humiliation channelled into telekinetic power. She starts punishing everyone who hurt her. *I really love when you get worked up like this.* Getting spurned is also a way of getting worked up, and getting worked up – in these pieces – is about so much more than appearing desirable to a lover: it's also about *getting the work up*, making something from lived experience. We hear a female voice say: 'Look at me,' and we see – in the bloody and punishing figure of Carrie – the expression of a deep rage at not being seen. We see the video itself as yet another claim on vision: *look at me.*

EVOKATION was the only piece in the Künstlerhaus installation in which Cantor's body or voice wasn't explicitly visible – and yet, there she was. The video shows glowing rivers of lava and fire juxtaposed with the footage from *CARRIE*, a bloody girl moving the objects of the world with every flick of her gaze – a constellation of bloody visions. These rivers summon a vision of bleeding that is also a vision of force and power.

In *PINOCHET PORN*, the unfinished feature-length film that Cantor was working on when she died of cancer in 2013, the question that keeps recurring, another kind of red castle across the film's frames, is a question about the relationship between pain and agency: *Is tragedy a choice?*

As a child, when Cantor visited the Detroit Institute of Art with her father, they always visited 'the same five pieces with the same commentary... our routine never varied.' They kept returning to the same works, just as her own work, years later, kept returning to certain sites of fascination – pain, blood, bodies, suffering, fire – the red castles of her psychic horizon line.

In the drawings that make up *CINDERELLA SYNDROME*, a sequence of her sketches framed on the wall in the gallery's final room, I found these preoccupations playing out as a kind of stick-figure soap opera. The sketches look like diary entries, all big feelings and messy lines: the narrative of an emotionally abusive marriage and a vision of domesticity curdled past saving. The installation takes its name from Colette Dowling's early-eighties notion of the 'Cinderella Complex', the unconscious female fear of independence and ingrained cultural fantasy of being saved by a man: 'Women are brought up to depend on a man and to feel naked and frightened without one,' Dowling wrote. 'We have been taught to believe that as females we cannot stand alone, that we are too fragile, too delicate, too needful of protection.' Cantor's drawings aren't an endorsement or a wholesale shaming of the desire to be taken care of; but they admit wrestling with this desire and its consequences.

In one drawing, a huge man – a grotesque vision of a husband – yells: 'YOU ARE AN IRRESPONSIBLE SELFISH BITCH!' from a messy oval mouth sketched in red and black, his eyes maniacal and bloodshot, his scribbled hand clutching the neck of a wife whose body has been drawn barely larger than his face, with two circles for boobs and a smile on her lips. Her speech bubble says simply: 'I'm sorry.'

The drawings insist that this terrible marriage is someone's vision of Happily-Ever-After. One drawing shows two parents saying 'WE ARE SO HAPPY ALL* ARE (sic) CHILDREN ARE MARRIED. (*EVEN OUR AWFUL STUPID UGLY DAUGHTER.)' But from the beginning of the series, the stupid ugly daughter is unwilling to submit herself entirely. The glass slipper of fairy tale never fits right. Her interior life – and her allegiance to that life – is a source of ongoing anxiety to her husband: 'Wot is she dreaming?' he wonders, leaning over her sleeping body. When he gets angry, their cats have her back: 'Leave her alone!' one says. The caption below them proudly declares: 'Led by Athena, the cats loved me.'

A few drawings later, the wife spends a summer at an artists' residency. This feels like freedom, leaving to make her art, but her husband isn't happy about it. He gets angry when she returns, and this time the cats take his side. They felt betrayed by her departure too. As he throttles her, they cheer: 'Go Mike!' The cats are like the comedic subplot in a Shakespearean tragedy, Thalia saying her piece. They are also

E

surrogates for the children Cantor never had. They were the ones she protected and sustained, or didn't. They were the ones she guiltily abandoned for the artistic life that sustained her.

When I saw messily-sketched Mike throttling his wife – *Go Mike!* – I thought of Pam writhing on her meathook. I thought of Sally begging for her life: 'You can stop him!' she yells to Leatherface's brother. I thought of Cantor's lover saying: *You're so obsessive and too heavy, and I like it* – the way a woman's intensity can be the source of her appeal, can make you want to have her, but it can also make it impossible to have her fully. *Wot is she dreaming?* I pictured that nightmare of a prom queen, playing just upstairs, dripping in blood. She was dreaming that.

When Cantor shifted away from large-scale paintings to work on 'small secret diary stories' in 1993, she didn't initially consider them artworks. She only displayed them after people 'strongly related to these intimate experiences', and convinced her to exhibit them. They were 'contextualised within the framework of feminism, that the personal is political', though she still 'feared that the work was also feminine in that it was discreet and diminutive'.

But facing these drawings in a gallery – drawings that felt raw, though I also felt their rawness as a deliberately crafted effect, their messy sketch-work framed behind glass – also made me aware of them as anything but diminutive. They insisted on finding a visual language for a painful marriage and a confined creative impulse, and they insisted that this representation was political, that the emotional life of an individual woman was also the site of multiple and powerful cultural forces converging: the pressure to be a certain kind of wife, the pressure to be a caregiver, the pressure to be available and legible in familiar ways, to refrain from dreaming too opaquely.

Instead, Cantor made herself legible in *un*familiar ways: as a set of spliced film clips and a set of cartoon drawings, a nun-bride and a slasher-film corpse-in-waiting. The woman in the *CINDERELLA SYNDROME* drawings was inscrutable and conflicted and deeply committed to her art, but she also refused to conform to heavy-handed feminist dogma. She wanted a partner and suffered under his influence. She also apologised to him, from fear or internalised guilt, and these feelings, desire and apology, were allowed into the frame as well. The woman in these drawings refused a kind of feminist narrative that might have wanted her *not* to want the man who treated her in these ways, that might have pushed her apologies and moments of weakness out of frame.

I was aware that these 'secret diary stories' were not diminutive insofar as they felt deeply connected to the rest of the installation. I could hear the sounds of a video from the other side of a white gallery wall, and I thought Cantor would be pleased by that. She once said she loved the way sound from one installation could spill over into

E

your experience of the artwork nearby. I could feel that happening – could feel these drawn scenes linked to the larger collage I found myself inside of, could feel their geometries in contact. Their presence refused the idea of the personal as *only* that, as sequestered.

I kept returning to the same red castle: a woman in pain, a woman on fire, those rivers of molten lava in EVOKATION OF MY DEMON SISTER. These women were hurting and making at once. They'd been wounded by love but they still believed in it. They didn't think the exclusion of pain was a prerequisite for the claiming of power. MY PERVERSION IS THE BELIEF IN TRUE LOVE is what Cantor called the only exhibit of video art she curated while she was still alive. Her work resisted bromides about love as a salvation story or a fairy tale, but it also refused to dismiss her desires just because they risked charges of naiveté or disempowerment.

Is tragedy a choice? The choice wasn't just about experience itself but about the genres in which experience might be recounted. And for Cantor, the question of genre was always a question of objects touching inside the frame she had built for them. When I watched her splice together footage of dream and nightmare, it summoned something like the emotional charge of objects touching in de Chirico – a blue rod and a red curve, or the forehead of a soldier and his wife, the juxtaposition of a smooth surface and a ragged one, the tension between a cluttered room and an open plaza. There was a kinship in the intensities she and de Chirico courted, though her intensities suggested narrative and his were based in geometries. But both were about unlike objects – or genres, or emotional states, or textures of paint – coming into contact. Cantor insisted on juxtaposing multiple moods in her vision of a broken heart. She insisted on bringing together the massacre and the music. She sought the pointy surfaces of disjunctive genres, their prick and sting – like shapes that didn't quite fit, like figures made of triangles still trying to embrace. Her own body in her work is something deeply crafted, never exposed; like another de Chirico body turning to pillar, ultimately revealing itself as form.

Cantor wanted to describe her love affair by showing a man with a chainsaw and a puppet show of goats, and I wanted to describe Cantor's 'vulnerability' as if it were some kind of Castello Estense, something I kept glimpsing in pieces and angled portions, through windows, incomplete and unavoidable – as if it were something I couldn't escape, and didn't want to. *I really love when you get worked up like this. You're so powerful.* The worked-up woman – a figure of farce and condescending desire, a descendant of hysterics. The worked-up woman – who got her work up, in the end.

IV.
On a Tuesday night, I read my essay about female pain in the corner of Künstlerhaus where the CINDERELLA SYNDROME drawings hung: drawings of Cantor's stick-figure

E

marriage, drawings of a woman getting throttled by her neck, drawings of a wife who was not one thing but many things (wife, daughter, artist, woman, dreamer, cat-owner) and who felt not one thing but many things (apologetic, inspired, wounded, resolute, powerful). The first question, once I finished reading, was not a question at all.

'I must confess that I have a lot of problems with the whole talk,' said a woman in the front row – tall and strongly built, with blonde hair and black slacks. I knew from the way she had smiled before she spoke that something bad was going to come out of her mouth. It wasn't a smile of pity, or regret. It was more tight-lipped. It held distaste.

She identified herself as a feminist immediately. She was in her mid-fifties, perhaps – old enough to be my young mother. She said she was tired of all these narratives of female suffering. 'When a middle class woman kind of *re-performs* the suffering,' she said, 'I think that's a very risky way to deal with that topic, I must say.'

I must say. It was like she'd found a dead mouse behind her stove, partly rotted, and had picked it up by its tail. She was trying to figure out how to throw it away. 'I would really claim,' she said, 'that people like you doing things like that – that kind of performance – is for me a bigger problem.'

People like you: I felt myself blushing. I felt myself start to sweat.

The German Feminist said that instead of simply offering more narratives of pain, I might want to ask *why* we found ourselves consuming these narratives or participating in them. She said, in fact, that she wasn't interested in narrative at all. She was interested in anti-narrative. I nodded, trying to seem unwounded and engaged, trying to seem razor-sharp. I had no idea what *anti-narrative* meant, or what she meant by it.

When it came to cutting, she said – she drew her fingers across her wrists, her expression full of disdain – perhaps I should think about why there 'is a specific moment in the patriarchy when people do that'.

I felt aware of the faint lines on my ankle – the internalisation of a patriarchy that had ostensibly made me feel inadequate or silenced enough to harm myself – and here was a woman's voice, doing the same thing, making me feel I shouldn't have spoken at all. It was as if describing pain – to her – was the same thing as saying there couldn't be anything *other* than pain. Talking about pain would always just mean re-performing it.

I waited quietly until she was done, or at least until she had paused. I said: 'I think your resistance is not actually in opposition to so many of the questions that the piece is after.' By which I meant: her anger was exactly what I'd been writing about.

I said I wanted to find a way to represent pain that didn't buy into familiar archetypes of suffering women.

'That's exactly my problem,' she said. 'That's exactly what always was... one

E

image that is presented again and again, women that suffer. I don't want a slightly new version of that. I think there must be many more possibilities.'

The Cantor video playing on the other side of the white gallery wall had a moment of dialogue – I knew, because I'd heard it earlier that day – in which one woman said to another: 'Everything is becoming easy, even overwhelming suffering.'

I responded, once again, by trying to agree with a woman determined to disagree with me: 'I believe in many narratives of what women do,' I told her, 'many narratives of how women live, what female identity can be constituted by.' I was like a woman who couldn't understand that she'd been rejected. I still wanted to be friends. I felt *narrative* come off my tongue like a dirty, stupid word. I couldn't help it.

As I spoke, the German Feminist started shaking her head. I kept going: I believed in multiplicity, I said, but I didn't think that a call for multiplicity meant we couldn't ever portray women's suffering. 'Perhaps that's where we have a fairly strong ethical divergence,' I said. But my voice trailed off and lilted up, into the needy swell of a question. I wasn't even sure what I meant by *ethical*, only that she and I disagreed. I hated my *perhaps*, and the implicit question mark in my voice, but also knew that in some basic – *perhaps* unrigorous way – I agreed with myself.

'I'm not interested in identity at all, honestly,' she said. 'I'm really interested in something else.'

In my mind I pictured a blackboard. ~~Narrative~~ and ~~Identity~~ had been written in chalk, and then crossed off: not allowed. There was so much this woman wasn't interested in. I wondered what interested her.

'I'm interested in being the split self in every moment,' she said, 'to try to unfold varieties. For example, a friend of mine told me that in giving birth she had the biggest orgasm of her life.'

I didn't know what to say to that. I only knew I was overwhelmed by the force of this woman's palpable disgust for me. It was like humidity in the air: her disgust for everything I'd come to represent for her over the course of an hour, my wound-mongering and wound-glorifying – the very things I'd wanted my essay to interrogate. When she looked at me – sitting in my knitted black dress, covered with knitted white skulls, the dress I'd worn to seem edgy, to poke fun at what it might mean to drape ourselves in damage, to wear it – all she saw was another woman beating the dead horse of hurting womanhood – *re-performing* it, like putting a half-eaten quiche back in the oven – damning us to such a thin slice of the representational pie.

I wanted to defend myself. But that isn't what I did. I said: 'I love that formulation of being a split self in every moment.' I said: 'I think that's quite beautiful. That resonates a lot for me.'

Part of me wanted to win whatever public argument we were having. But another part of me just wanted to win her approval. I wanted to be seen and respected, to be *enough.* I kept thinking about Carrie covered in blood, in Cantor's video, and the voice saying: *Look at me. Look at me. Look at me.* It felt vaguely pathetic, to sit up there and call this woman's phrase beautiful while she dismissed every word coming out of my mouth. I remembered something Cantor had once said – *I think my artworks can really be misconstrued* – like fondling a talisman in my pocket.

In the German Feminist's disdain, and in the force of her self-assurance, I felt her truth become my truth. This had happened to me before. I could feel so porous to another person's appraisal of me. I could feel swallowed by it. *Is tragedy a choice?* I felt like I'd failed feminism by choosing the tragic. I felt myself throttled around the neck by huge hands, my speech bubble squeaking: 'I'm sorry.' The hands around my neck belonged to a woman, not a man, but this somehow only made it worse – as if she'd recreated some version of the power structures I'd come to associate with women pandering to men, with *me* pandering to men: the struggle to be good enough, speak well enough, acquit myself.

Near the end of the night, the gallery curator turned to me and asked: 'Should we take any more questions?' The German Feminist was the only person in the audience with her hand up, ready to speak again. The curator was giving me a choice: Was I willing to take more of it from her? I said: 'Sure.'

That moment interests me, my *sure.* It was a kind of masochism – wanting the flagellation, wanting to know all the ways I was inadequate – in the eyes of a woman older than me, a woman more confrontational than me, a woman who had read more theory than me. I needed the fullest version of the ritual whipping. When I told her that her anger was precisely what my writing was *about,* I could hear how feeble my voice sounded, how conciliatory, as if I were kneeling in front of her, a supplicant, saying: *See, look. I did what you told me to do, even if you think I failed at it.* As if I were pleading my case: *I didn't want to fail your feminism, I promise.*

She spoke three times in total – as if we were caught in some primal shaming ritual, three stones she would throw at me in the village square, an elder woman hazing a younger one. The last time she spoke, she listed all the theorists she thought I needed to read, like I'd been bad and she was telling me how many Hail Marys I needed to recite. I imagined our encounter spliced with scenes from *THE TEXAS CHAINSAW MASSACRE*: toggling back and forth between my evisceration and Pam dangling from a meat hook; between my pandering and Sally's pleading at the dinner table: *You can stop him!*

There was something ridiculous and hilarious about how the German Feminist made me feel, about how much she made me feel – how outsized it felt, her disdain and my crumpling in response. It made me grateful for the work all around us, and how Cantor recognised the absurdity and hilarity and largeness of moving through the world as a feeling person – how she wasn't ashamed to document the size of feeling,

E

and the way it sought associations and attachments. She wasn't ashamed of the hubris of juxtaposition. She wasn't ashamed to make fun of how raw the nerves become when confronted by a face made of leather or indifference.

At a certain point, as I was responding to her third and final monologue, the German Feminist turned away from me entirely, pointedly, so fully I could see her face in profile, the tendons taut in her neck. This only made me want to keep talking. Her dismissal only made me think that if I spoke enough, or spoke well enough, I could pull her gaze back to meet mine.

This was before she told me to read Emmanuel Levinas, whose philosophy begins in the face-to-face encounter. 'The face speaks to me,' he wrote, 'and thereby invites me to a relation.' For Levinas, the face is what makes us aware of our primal obligations to one another. He describes it in terms of its 'upright exposure, without defence. The skin of the face is that which stays most naked, most destitute.'

For years, I had hated the word *vulnerability*. For years, I had hated the presumption that my creative work was somehow predicated on exposure, and I'd hated the implication that I was asking for something – sympathy, commiseration, adulation, whatever – when I shared this work with the world.

For years, I had hated the word *vulnerability*. But once the German feminist was done with me, I went into a German bathroom stall and cried.

V.

Later that night, I told my husband about the German Feminist over Skype. I told him about everything she wasn't interested in. I told him that her friend had experienced childbirth as the biggest orgasm of her life. When he said, 'I don't think her friend's been having sex right,' it made me laugh. It made me wish he'd been in the room to make his joke in front of everyone. It made me wish he'd been in the room to tell the German Feminist: *That's enough. You need to stop.* I imagined him doing all the things I hadn't been able to do. He would have told the woman she was being disrespectful, that she needed to stop talking, that her friend wouldn't know an orgasm from a car accident.

If only he'd been there, I thought, to say the things I couldn't. *We have been taught to believe that as females we cannot stand alone, that we are too fragile, too delicate, too needful of protection.* It was my own Cinderella Complex – needing him there, wishing he could have defended me the way I couldn't defend myself.

After the German Feminist's final monologue, a conceptual artist sitting beside her raised his hand. He didn't have a question, either. But his question-without-a-question-mark was about the virtues of uncertainty. He said he appreciated the way my work proceeded from a place of unknowing. He kept using the word naïveté. I felt grateful and ashamed at once – grateful that he had felt there was something valuable

E

about anything I'd said, ashamed that I needed his defence, and even *more* ashamed that I was being defended by a man who was praising my work for being naïve.

When I consider the Conceptual Artist's defence, or what he meant to praise, I remember de Chirico's interest in the minds of children. Many of his paintings reproduced views from the bedroom windows of his childhood, showing only those parts of a train that he could see from his short height. His 1916 painting THE LANGUAGE OF A CHILD frames a simple arrangement of objects – rolled-up papers and bread shaped like the X you might find on a treasure map – but its simplicity also feels carefully crafted to ask what might be useful and generative about seeing things as a child sees them – to bring together what others might not think belongs together, or matters enough to display. When I consider the Conceptual Artist's defence, I think of James Baldwin, who once wrote: 'The purpose of art is to lay bare the questions that have been hidden by the answers.'

That night, I agreed with the Conceptual Artist about the generative virtues of uncertainty. But I didn't want to defend myself as a child. I wanted to defend myself as a woman. I wanted to defend myself as a woman who insisted, as Cantor had insisted, that admitting pain didn't preclude the possibility of claiming power. I felt her drawings in the room around us, felt her films playing above us, and I wanted to be saved by them, a desire that was perhaps somehow kin to the complex they were named for – *too fragile, too delicate, too needful of protection.* I thought of those two cats in the corner of one of her drawings, shouting: *Leave her alone!* I wanted to say that admitting pain doesn't mean reducing yourself to it, that describing the pain of others doesn't mean reducing *them* to it. I wanted to say that Cantor's art – to me – felt like the perfect expression of a necessary simultaneity: pain and power at once. I found comfort and sustenance and generative possibility and even a weird kind of forgiveness in the recurring castles of her preoccupations: *Is tragedy a choice? Everything is becoming easy, even overwhelming suffering.* The woman on the meat hook. The bloody girl on stage. *Fucking hell, is there no way out of this?*

I wondered if every woman who had ever felt childbirth as something painful had somehow failed us all, by giving us a version of the pain story we'd already heard. I was interested in the woman who experienced giving birth as an orgasm, and I was also interested in the woman who didn't. That *also*, more than anything, came to seem like the crucial difference between me and the German Feminist, but perhaps it's self-serving to frame it that way, a flash of *l'esprit d'escalier* that keeps elbowing into view. De Chirico's figures were composed of many shapes, and I wanted to believe that a woman could be composed of many shapes as well – that this could be confessed without understanding any of these shapes as totalising truth. *The self split in every moment.* Was it cowardly or pandering to feel there were certain ways the German Feminist and I agreed? I felt that Cantor's work made a case for the *also* of pain alongside

E

other states of feeling, pain alongside various iterations of desire: lust, caregiving, and the impulse to create. Her work made space for Thalia and Melpomene – the muses of tragedy and comedy, forever facing away from each other in de Chirico's plaza – in its heartbreak and its bloodbaths and its peanut gallery of cats: *Leave her alone!* 'My work is humorous,' Cantor once said, 'but also quite disturbing.'

I thought of those muses – each stone woman rigidly defending her own art, neither one facing the other – and wondered what made them so disquieting. Perhaps it was their stiff posture, or their inscrutable bodies, their awkward lack of relation to one another; or perhaps it was that their heads had no faces, and the face is how we begin to understand what we owe each other. In 'The Disquieting Muses', Sylvia Plath writes of her 'dismal-headed / Godmothers', each one 'Mouthless, eyeless, with stitched bald head', who stand their 'vigils in gowns of stone, / Faces blank as the day I was born'.

I was born two years before THE CINDERELLA COMPLEX, a decade after THE TEXAS CHAINSAW MASSACRE, and a decade before Cantor spliced it into her own kind of song. I was born into a culture that had already metabolised certain ideas about the suffering woman as an emblem of female disenfranchisement. When I felt taken to task by the German Feminist, I also felt taken to task by the ghosts of feminism(s) past – the ghosts of forces who had fought hard for women to be seen as more than weak, suffering figures who wanted or needed to be defended. The truth was, I did not understand myself as undermining their fight but extending it. Reckoning with her muses, Plath wrote: 'This is the kingdom you bore me to, / Mother, mother, but no frown of mine / Will betray the company I keep.'

Plath felt she'd been born into the ranks of 'stitched bald' female heads, that she was expected to be a particular kind of woman, a particular kind of mother, a particular kind of wife – and that these expectations asked her, among other things, not to frown too much. When I betrayed nothing on stage, when I said *sure*, I'd take a little more abuse, I told myself this was strength. If I believed in dissecting vulnerability rather than enacting it, I needed to betray nothing. The stone-faced goddess has perpetuated certain myths of her own. *I prefer a little more stoicism*, a male critic had once said of my book, and all its wounds. When I said, sure, I'd take another question, I was trying to be stoic – trying to be the opposite of vulnerable.

I didn't start crying until I closed the latch on the gallery bathroom stall, and when I passed the German Feminist in the gallery stairwell later, as we went our separate ways into the night, I felt my face deforming itself into a hopelessly ingratiating smile. I had no *esprit d'escalier* then. I felt how we wanted the same things, for ourselves and all our godmothers in the plaza, how we craved a certain suppleness and infinitude of consciousness, *the split self at every moment* – and also how we stood, with our arms crossed and our stone gowns, and couldn't speak to one another right. I wanted to

E

know where and when I'd learned to smile at the people I felt I'd failed, and where and when I'd learned to believe each one, how I'd learned to feel inadequate through their collective gaze.

It felt good to sit on a bare toilet in a locked bathroom stall – did the Germans believe in toilet lids? – and not say anything to anyone. I decided it would be more comfortable to be the muse of comedy than the muse of tragedy – in de Chirico's everlasting vista – because at least Thalia got to sit down. Melpomene had to stand there in her rippled stone gown until the fucking *end of time*, with the sun never setting, the illumination never letting up.

That night, after the event was done, I went to dinner with an artist who carried his own wicker chair through the darkened streets of Stuttgart, all the way to Marienplatz, where four of us sat at a table that only had three chairs, and *voilà*. He had what we needed. This artist said de Chirico had written beautifully about the difference between seated and standing figures. I thought of Melpomene on guard; I thought of Thalia at rest. I thought of the strange hilarity of *spilling your guts* about a love affair – the critical language about female confessional work that always takes refuge in the body – while Leatherface spilled the guts of women on screen. I thought about why I'd always hated *vulnerability*, the way it confused craft with exposure, and whether I'd confirmed the German Feminist's critique by crying in a bathroom stall after she'd levelled it at me, whether I'd revealed myself as little more than the leakage of tears arranged across a page, or performed in front of an audience.

I felt so disappointed in myself – not in the ideas I'd presented but in the ways I'd failed to defend them, the ways in which a woman's dismissal had only compelled me more forcefully toward the imperative of proving myself to her. In wanting to prove myself to her, I also wanted to prove myself worthy of the space, and Cantor's art inside the space. I wanted to believe that crying in a bathroom stall didn't mean I'd replaced Cantor's rigorous vision of vulnerability with something more predictable and retrograde, something obviously weak.

It was there with me in that stall, *vulnerability*, part of my experience even if I hadn't wanted to claim it. Of course there was vulnerability in bringing any idea into the world, in saying anything you meant. Of course there was vulnerability in being made of something besides stone. Of course there was vulnerability in having faith in uncertainty and its generative potential. The question mark of uncertainty was more than just a convenient intellectual alibi; it could leave you feeling exposed in that empty plaza. It could bring you to a locked stall, sitting on a toilet, feeling yourself overwhelmed by the self you had become to another pair of eyes – the eyes that looked away, whose gaze you kept courting anyway.

Is tragedy a choice? Tragedy stands in her stone gown forever. She stands in the kingdom I was born to, but she doesn't stand there alone. *Wot is she dreaming?* She dreams heaven and hell. She dreams them both. *The face speaks to me and thereby invites me to a relation.* Her face isn't human, not in that plaza, but in the dream and in the nightmare I could hear her voice: *Look at me.* Look.

E

SPONSORS

[+]

Anna Susanna Woof
Natural Presentation
September 30th - November 12th 2016

| SUNDAY Art Fair
October 6th - 9th 2016
Rachal Bradley, Samuel Jeffery, Jan Vorisek

---   [−]

Dépossession
Nayland Blake, Nate Boyce, Christophe de Rohan Chabot,
Timothy Davies, Brendan Fowler, Andrew Munks.
December 2nd - January 21st 2017

---   [+]

Jacqueline Fraser
THE MAKING OF A MOST VIOLENT YEAR 2017
February 3rd - March 18th 2017

Remko Scha   [+]
March 31st - May 13th 2017

[] Jan Vorisek
June 2nd - July 15th 2017

|

TG   [−]

33 Seely Road   Nottingham   NG7 1NU   UK   www.tgal.co

Alice Walton
Almost All the Girls Raise Their Hands
2 November – 3 December 2016

107 Essex Road, London, N1 2SL
www.tintypegallery.com

TINTYPE

THE WHITE REVIEW

SUBSCRIBE!

20 per cent off all back issues, using the code CHELSEAGIRLS

Offer expires 31 December 2016

www.thewhitereview.org

Uri Aran
September 2016
62 Kingly Street

David Korty
September 2016
1 Davies Street

Borna Sammak
October 2016
9 Balfour Mews

Laura Owens
October 2016
62 Kingly Street

Sadie Coles HQ
1 Davies Street London W1K 3DB
62 Kingly Street London W1B 5QN

www.sadiecoles.com

Sadie Coles   HQ

SPUR

SPUR

New winter commissions:
Jennifer Mehigan
Georgia Lucas-Going

SPUR is a research-led contemporary arts
commissioning organisation based in the North of England.

www.spurspurspur.org

Bloomberg
New
Contemporaries
2016

Selected by Anya Gallaccio,
Alan Kane and Haroon Mirza

ICA, London
ica.org.uk
22 November 2016 –
26 January 2017

newcontemporaries.org.uk
info@newcontemporaries.org.uk
🐦 @NewContemps
📘 New Contemporaries
📷 @newcontemps

Supported by:

ICA   **New Contemporaries**

LOVELIFE

Jonathan Baldock and Emma Hart an Exhibition in 3 Acts

PEER, LONDON – NOV 2016 TO JAN 2017.
PEERUK.ORG

GRUNDY ART GALLERY, BLACKPOOL – JUNE TO AUG 2017.
GRUNDYARTGALLERY.COM

DE LA WARR PAVILION, BEXHILL ON SEA – OCT TO DEC 2017.
DLWP.COM

PEER   GRUNDY ART GALLERY   DE LA WARR PAVILION

Supported by
The National Lottery®
through Arts Council England

ARTS COUNCIL
ENGLAND

WERNER SCHREIB
AND ANNEA LOCKWOOD

AFTERSHOCK The Grammar of Silence

curated by Rozemin Keshvani

17 September–12 November 2016

Opening hours Wed–Sat, 1–6pm

2 Hanway Place | London | W1T 1HB

laure**genillard**

lglondoninfo@gmail.com | www.lglondon.org
+44 (0)2073232327 | +44 (0)7796156805

New from Sylph Editions

To Begin at the Beginning
JAVIER MARÍAS

Translated and with an Essay by Margaret Jull Costa

"Marías is forever redrawing the thin line that separates illusion from reality."—*Paris Review*

Paper £13.50

The Story Smuggler
GEORGI GOSPODINOV

With Illustrations by Theodore Ushev

"Gospodinov's model is Borges, whose delight in mischievous games and extravagant fantasy he shares."—*New Yorker*

Paper £13.50

Going Bush
KIRSTY GUNN

"Gunn's language is pitch-perfect."—*New York Times Book Review*

Paper £13.50

Distributed by the University of Chicago Press
www.press.uchicago.edu

London

Regent's Park
6–9 October 2016
New Preview Day
Wednesday 5 October

Tickets at frieze.com

FRIEZE ART FAIR

Arch designed by James Stirling. Image selection: Pablo Bronstein. Photography Luke Hayes.

Media partner

FINANCIAL
TIMES

Main sponsor
Deutsche Bank

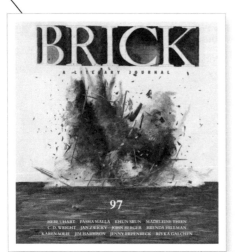

In *Brick* 97

John Berger
Rivka Galchen
Madeleine Thien
Jan Zwicky
Miron Białoszewski
Jenny Erpenbeck
Karen Solie
Pasha Malla
Order yours at BrickMag.com

BRICK
A LITERARY JOURNAL

Edited by Michael Helm, Linda Spalding,
Laurie D Graham, Rebecca Silver Slayter, and Martha Sharpe

Art
MONTHLY

Taking art apart since 1976

Subscription offer for White Review readers
www.artmonthly.co.uk/whitereview2016

NOON

A LITERARY ANNUAL

1324 LEXINGTON AVENUE   PMB 298   NEW YORK NY 10128

EDITION PRICE $12 DOMESTIC $17 FOREIGN

APPENDIX

OSAMA ALOMAR was born in Damascus, Syria, in 1968, and now lives in Chicago. He is the author of three collections of short stories and a volume of poetry. He is a regular contributor to various newspapers and journals within the Arab world. *THE TEETH OF THE COMB & OTHER STORIES*, excerpted here, will be published by New Directions in 2017.

MICHAEL BARRON is a writer and editor based in New York.

C. J. COLLINS is a librarian and translator based in Queens, New York.

RYE DAG HOLMBOE is a writer and teaching fellow in the History of Art Department at University College London. His writings have appeared in *THE WHITE REVIEW*, *ART LICKS*, *APOLLO* and in academic journals.

MARIA DIMITROVA is a writer based in London.

JEN GEORGE was born in Thousand Oaks, California. She lives and works in New York City. Her first book, *THE BABYSITTER AT REST*, is published by the Dorothy Project in October 2016.

YANYAN HUANG was born in Sichuan, China. She currently lives and works between Italy, China, and California. She studied her Bachelor of Arts at the University of California Los Angeles. Her work has been exhibited internationally.

LESLIE JAMISON is the author of a novel, *THE GIN CLOSET*, and a collection of essays, *THE EMPATHY EXAMS*. Her work has appeared in *HARPER'S*, *OXFORD AMERICAN*, *A PUBLIC SPACE*, *VIRGINIA QUARTERLY REVIEW*, and *THE BELIEVER*. She is a columnist for the *NEW YORK TIMES BOOK REVIEW*, and an Assistant Professor at Columbia University. She lives in Brooklyn with her family.

LEE KLEIN's fiction, essays, reviews, and translations have appeared in *HARPER'S*, *THE BEST AMERICAN NONREQUIRED READING 2007*, and many other sites, journals, and anthologies. He translated *REVULSION: THOMAS BERNHARD IN SAN SALVADOR* by Horacio Castellanos Moya (New Directions, 2016). He lives in South Philadelphia.

DENISE KUPFERSCHMIDT received her BFA from Massachusetts College of Art in Boston. Recent solo exhibitions have been with Halsey McKay Gallery, Left Field Gallery, San Luis Obispo, The Ace Hotel, NY and Cooper Cole Gallery, Toronto. Her work has been included in numerous group exhibitions, including Magenta Plains, BAM's Next Wave Festival, Foxy Production, Eleven Rivington, Nicole Klagsbrun and Tracey Williams, NY, amongst others. She was an organiser of the itinerant group-show series Apartment Show, has been included in *MODERN PAINTERS* 100 Artists to Watch and was a 2010 NADA Emerging Artist. Kupferschmidt is represented by Halsey McKay Gallery.

DOROTHEA LASKY is the author of four full-length collections of poetry: *ROME* (Liveright/W. W. Norton), as well as *THUNDERBIRD*, *BLACK LIFE*, and *AWE*. She has also written several chapbooks, including *POETRY IS NOT A PROJECT* (Ugly Ducking Presse, 2010). Her writing has appeared in *POETRY*, *THE NEW YORKER*, *THE PARIS REVIEW*, *THE ATLANTIC*, and *BOSTON REVIEW*, among other places. She is a co-editor of *OPEN THE DOOR*: *HOW TO EXCITE YOUNG PEOPLE ABOUT POETRY* (McSweeney's, 2013). She is an Assistant Professor of Poetry at Columbia University's School of the Arts and lives in New York City.

ROSANNA MCLAUGHLIN is a writer and curator based in London. She has written for *FRIEZE* and *BOMB MAGAZINE*.

MOONI PERRY is a London-based artist from South Korea. She received her BA from Hogik University, Seoul prior to studying on the MA Painting programme at the Royal College of Art. She is currently working on an ongoing project, 'Floating with Other Artists'. In July 2016 her work was exhibited at the Liverpool Biennale as part of the Bloomberg New Contemporaries exhibition, which will open at the ICA London in November 2016.

SAM RIVIERE is the author of the poetry collections *81 AUSTERITIES* (Faber, 2012), *STANDARD TWIN FANTASY* (Egg Box, 2014), and *KIM KARDASHIAN'S MARRIAGE* (Faber, 2015), and an 'unprintable book', *THE TRUTH ABOUT CATS AND DOGS* (Visual Editions, 2016), with Joe Dunthorne. He also runs the micropublisher If a Leaf Falls Press.

SALLY ROONEY is a writer living in Dublin. Her work has appeared in *GRANTA*, *THE DUBLIN REVIEW* and *THE STINGING FLY*. Her first novel, *CONVERSATIONS WITH FRIENDS*, is due out in 2017 from Faber & Faber.

FRIENDS OF THE WHITE REVIEW

AARON BOGART

ABI MITCHELL

ABIGAIL YUE WANG

ADAM FREUDENHEIM

ADAM HALL

ADAM SAUNBY

ADELINE DE MONSEIGNAT

AGRI ISMAIL

AJ DEHANY

ALAN MURRIN

ALBA ZIEGLER-BAILEY

ALBERT BUCHARD

ALEX GREINER

ALEX MCDONALD

ALEX MCELROY

ALEXA MITTERHUBER

ALICE OSWALD

ALIX MCCAFFREY

AMBIKA SUBRAMANIAM

AMI GREKO

AMY SHERLOCK

ANASTASIA SVOBODA

ANASTASIA VIKHORNOVA

AND OTHER STORIES

ANDREW CURRAN

ANDREW LELAND

ANDREW ROADS

ANNA DELLA SUBIN

ANNA WHITE

ANNE MEADOWS

ANNE WALTON

ARCHIPELAGO BOOKS

ARIANNE LOVELACE

ARIKE OKE

ASIA LITERARY AGENCY

AUDE FOURGOUS

BAPTISTE VANPOULLE

BARBARA HORIUCHI

BARNEY WALSH

BEN HINSHAW

BEN LERNER

BEN POLLNER

BERNADETTE EASTHAM

BOOK/SHOP

BRIAN WILLIAMS

BRIGITTE HOLLWEG

BROOMBERG & CHANARIN

CAMILLE GAJEWSKI

CAMILLE HENROT

CARLOTTA EDEN

CAROL HUSTON

CAROLINE LANGLEY

CAROLINE YOUNGER

CAROLYN LEK

CARRIE ETTER

CATHERINE HAMILTON

CERI JANE WEIGHTMAN

CHARLES LUTYENS

CHARLIE HARKIN

CHARLOTTE COHEN

CHARLOTTE GRACE

CHEE LUP WAN

CHINA MIÉVILLE

CHISENHALE GALLERY

CHRIS KRAUS

CHRIS WEBB

CHRISTIAN LORENTZEN

CHRISTOPHER GRAY

CJ CAREY

CLAIRE DE DIVONNE

CLAIRE DE ROUEN

CLAIRE-LOUISE BENNETT

CLAUDE ADJIL

CODY STUART

CONOR DELAHUNTY

COSMO LANDESMAN

CRISTOBAL BIANCHI

CYNTHIA & WILLIAM MORRISON-BELL

CYRILLE GONZALVES

DANIEL COHEN

DANIELA BECHLY

DANIELA SUN

DAVID AND HARRIET POWELL

DAVID ANDREW

DAVID BARNETT

DAVID BREUER

DAVID EASTHAM

DAVID ROSE

DAVID THORNE

DEBORAH LEVY

DEBORAH SMITH

DES LLOYD BEHARI

DEV KARAN AHUJA

DOUGLAS CANDANO

DR GEORGE HENSON

DR SAM NORTH

ED BROWNE

ED CUMMING

EDDIE REDMAYNE

EDWARD GRACE

ELEANOR CHANDLER

ELEY WILLIAMS

ELIAS FECHER

ELSPETH MITCHELL

EMILY BUTLER

EMILY LUTYENS

EMILY RUDGE

EMMA WARREN

ENRICO TASSI

EPILOGUE

EUAN MONAGHAN

EUGENIA LAPTEVA

EUROPA EDITIONS

EVA KELLENBERGER

FABER & FABER

FABER ACADEMY

FABER MEMBERS

FANNY SINGER

FATOS USTEK

FIONA GEILINGER

FIONA GRADY

FITZCARRALDO EDITIONS

FLORA CADZOW

FOLIO SOCIETY

FOUR CORNERS BOOKS

FRANCESCO PEDRAGLIO

GABRIEL VOGT

GALLAGHER LAWSON

GARY HABER

GEORGE HICKS

GEORGETTE TESTARD

GEORGIA GRIFFITHS

GEORGIA LANGLEY

GERMAN SIERRA

GHISLAIN DE RINCQUESEN

GILDA WILLIAMS

GILLIAN GRANT

GLENN BURTON

GRANTA BOOKS

HANNAH BARRY

HANNAH NAGLE

HANNAH WESTLAND

HANS ULRICH OBRIST

HARRIET HOROBIN-WORLEY

HARRY ECCLES-WILLIAMS

HARRY VAN DE BOSPOORT

HATTIE FOSTER

HAYLEY DIXON

HEADMASTER MAGAZINE

HELEN BARRELL

HELEN PYE

HELEN THORNE

HEMAN CHONG

HENRIETTTA SPIEGELBERG

HENRY HARDING

HENRY MARTIN

HENRY WRIGHT

HIKARI YOKOYAMA

HONEY LUARD

HORATIA HARROD

HOW TO ACADEMY

IAIN BROOME

IAN CHUNG

ICA

ISELIN SKOGLI

JACOB GARDNER

JACQUES STRAUSS

JADE FRENCH

JADE KOCH

JAMES BROOKES

JAMES KING

JAMES MEWIS

JAMES PUSEY

JAMES TURNBULL

JASPER ZAGAET

JAYA PRADHAN

JEANNE CONSTANS

JENNIFER CUSTER

JENNIFER HAMILTON-EMERY

JEREMY ADDISON

JEREMY DELLER

JEREMY MOULTON

JES FERNIE

JESSICA CRAIG

JESSICA SANTASCOY

JIAN WEI LIM

JO COLLEY

JOANNA WALSH

JOHN GORDON

JOHN LANGLEY

JOHN MURRAY

JOHN SCANLAN

JOHN SCHANCK

JOHN SIMNETT

JON DAY

FRIENDS OF THE WHITE REVIEW

JONATHAN CAPE
JONATHAN DUNCAN
JONATHAN WILLIAMS
JORDAN BASS
JORDAN HUMPHREYS
JORDAN RAZAVI
JORDI CARLES SUBIRA
JOSEPH DE LACEY
JOSEPH EDWARD
JOSEPHINE NEW
JOSHUA COHEN
JOSHUA DAVIS
JUDY BIRKBECK
JULIA CRABTREE
JULIA DINAN
JULIE PACHICO
JULIEN BÉZILLE
JURATE GACIONYTE
JUSTIN JAMES WALSH
KAJA MURAWSKA
KAMIYE FURUTA
KATE BRIGGS
KATE LOFTUS-O'BRIEN
KATE WILLS
KATHERINE LOCKTON
KATHERINE RUNDELL
KATHERINE TEMPLAR LEWIS
KATHRYN MARIS
KATHRYN SIEGEL
KEENAN MCCRACKEN
KIERAN CLANCY
KIERAN RID
KIRSTEEN HARDIE
KIT BUCHAN
KYLE PARKER
LAURA SNOAD
LAUREN ELKIN
LEAH SWAIN
LEE JORDAN
LEON DISCHE BECKER
LEWIS BUNGENER
LIA TEN BRINK
LIAM ROGERS
LILI HAMLYN
LILLIPUT PRESS
L'IMPOSSIBLE
LITERARY KITCHEN
LORENZ KLINGEBIEL
LOUISE GUINNESS
LOZANA ROSSENOVA
LUCIA PIETROIUSTI
LUCIE ELVEN
LUCY KUMARA MOORE
LUISA DE LANCASTRE
LUIZA SAUMA
MACK
MACLEHOSE PRESS
MAJDA GAMA
MALTE KOSIAN
MARIA DIMITROVA
MARIANNA SIMNETT
MARILOU TESTARD
MARIS KREIZMAN
MARK EL-KHATIB
MARK KROTOV

MARKUS ZETT
MARTA ARENAL LLORENTE
MARTIN CREED
MARTIN NICHOLAS
MATHILDE CABANAS
MATT GOLD
MATT HURCOMB
MATT MASTRICOVA
MATTHEW BALL
MATTHEW JOHNSTON
MATTHEW PONSFORD
MATTHEW RUDMAN
MAX FARRAR
MAX PORTER
MAX YOUNGMAN
MAXIME DARGAUD-FONS
MEGAN PIPER
MELISSA GOLDBERG
MELVILLE HOUSE
MICHAEL GREENWOLD
MICHAEL HOLTMANN
MICHAEL LEUE
MICHAEL SIGNORELLI
MICHAEL TROUGHTON
MICHELE SNYDER
MILES JOHNSON
MINIMONIOTAKU
MIRIAM GORDIS
MONICA OLIVEIRA
MONICA TIMMS
NAOMI CHANNA
NATHAN BRYANT
NATHAN FRANCIS
NED BEAUMAN
NEDA NEYNSKA
NEIL D.A. STEWART
NEW DIRECTIONS
NICK MULGREW
NICK SKIDMORE
NICK VOSS
NICKY BEAVEN
NICOLA SMYTH
NICOLAS CHAUVIN
NICOLE SIBELET
NILLY VON BAIBUS
OLEKSIY OSNACH
OLGA GROTOVA
OLI JACOBS
OLIVER BASCIANO
OLIVIA HEAL
OLIVIER RICHON
ONEWORLD
ORLANDO WHITFIELD
OSCAR GAYNOR
OWEN BOOTH
ØYSTEIN W ARBO
PADDY KELLY
PANGAEA SCULPTORS CENTRE
PATRICK GODDARD
PATRICK HAMM
PATRICK RAMBAUD
PATRICK STAFF
PAUL KEEGAN
PAUL TEASDALE
PEDRO

PEIRENE PRESS
PENGUIN BOOKS
PETER MURRAY
PHILIBERT DE DIVONNE
PHILIP JAMES MAUGHAN
PHILLIP KIM
PHOEBE STUBBS
PICADOR
PIERRE TESTARD
PIERS BARCLAY
PRIMORDIAL SEA
PUSHKIN PRESS
RACHEL ANDREWS
RACHEL GRACE
REBECCA SERVADIO
RENÄTE PRANCÄNE
RENATUS WU
RHYS TIMSON
RICHARD GLUCKMAN
RICHARD WENTWORTH
ROB SHARP
ROB SHERWOOD
ROBERT O'MEARA
ROBIN CAMERON
ROC SANDFORD
RORY O'KEEFFE
ROSALIND FURNESS
ROSANNA BOSCAWEN
ROSE BARCLAY
ROSIE CLARKE
RUBY COWLING
RUPERT CABBELL MANNERS
RUPERT MARTIN
RYAN CHAPMAN
RYAN EYERS
SADIE SMITH
SALLY BAILEY
SALLY MERCER
SALVAGE MAGAZINE
SAM BROWN
SAM GORDON
SAM MOSS
SAM SOLNICK
SAM THORNE
SAMUEL HUNT
SANAM GHARAGOZLOU
SARA BURNS
SARAH HARDIE
SARAH Y. VARNAM
SASKIA VOGEL
SCOTT ESPOSITO
SEAN HOOD
SEB EASTHAM
SELF PUBLISH, BE HAPPY
SERPENTINE GALLERY
SERPENT'S TAIL
SHARMAINE LOVEGROVE
SHOOTER LITERARY MAGAZINE
SIMON HARPER
SIMON WILLIAMS
SIMONE SCHRÖDER
SJOERD KRUIKEMEIER
SK THALE
SKENDER GHILAGA
SOPHIE CUNDALE

FRIENDS OF THE WHITE REVIEW

SOUMEYA ROBERTS
SOUTH LONDON GALLERY
SPIKE ISLAND
STEFANOS KOKOTOS
STEPHANIE TURNER
STEVE FLETCHER
SUSAN TOMASELLI
TAYLOR LE MELLE
TED MARTIN GREIJER
TELMO PRODUCCIONES
TERRIN WINKEL
THE ALARMIST
THE APPROACH
THE LETTER PRESS
THE REAL MATT WRIGHT
THEA HAWLIN
THEA URDAL
THEMISTOKLIS GIOKROUSSIS
THIBAULT CABANAS
THOMAS BUNSTEAD
THOMAS FRANCIS
THOMAS MOHR
THREE STAR BOOKS
TIM CURTAIN
TIMOTHY RENNIE
TITOUAN RUSSO
TOM GRACE
TOM JONES
TOM MCCARTHY
TROLLEY BOOKS
TZE-WEN CHAO
VALERIE BONNARDEL
VANESSA NICHOLAS
VERONIQUE TESTARD
VERSO BOOKS
VICTORIA MCGEE
VICTORIA MIRO
VIKTOR TIMOFEEV
VITA PEACOCK
WAYNE DALY
WEFUND.CO.UK
WHITE CUBE
WILL
WILL CHANCELLOR
WILL HEYWARD
WILL PALLEY
WILL SELF
WILLIAM ALDERWICK
WILLIAM CAIRNS
WILLOW GOLD
YASMINE SEALE
ZAYNAB DENA ZIARI
ZOE PILGER
ZOYA ROUS